THE CENTURY
THAT WAS

THE CENTURY THAT WAS

Reflections on
the Last One
Hundred Years

EDITED AND WITH AN

INTRODUCTION BY

James Cross Giblin

ATHENEUM BOOKS FOR YOUNG READERS

NEW YORK · LONDON · TORONTO · SYDNEY · SINGAPORE

Atheneum Books for Young Readers

An imprint of Simon & Schuster Children's Publishing Division

1230 Avenue of the Americas, New York, New York 10020

2   4   6   8   10   9   7   5   3   1

Library of Congress Cataloging-in-Publishing Data

The century that was : reflections on the last one hundred years /

edited and with an introduction by James Cross Giblin.—1st ed.

p.   cm.

Includes bibliographical references (p.) and index.

Summary: A collection of essays by well-known authors for young people, reflecting on various aspects of life in twentieth-century America, including politics, the environment, sports, fashion, and civil rights.

ISBN 0-689-82281-2

1.United States—Civilization—20th century Juvenile literature. 2. American essays Juvenile literature. [1. United States—Civilization—20th century.] I. Giblin, James.

E169.1.C39   2000   973.91—dc21   99-27011

FIRST EDITION

CONTENTS

INTRODUCTION

When the twentieth century began, the most popular magazine for young people was *St. Nicholas*. Its readership covered a broad age span, from boys and girls in elementary school to young adults of sixteen and seventeen. Its content ranged just as widely and included short stories, myths, legends, poems, and articles about everything from anteaters to the newfangled automobile.

Curious to see how *St. Nicholas* celebrated the start of the new century, I turned to the January 1900 issue—and discovered that I was a year early. Mary Mapes Dodge, the magazine's editor (or "conductor," as she preferred to call herself), explained why in a note to her readers. "Many regard 1900 as marking the first year of a new century, though this is not really the case," Mrs. Dodge wrote. "The first century began with the first year of the Christian era, A.D. 1. The first year of the twentieth century will begin with the year 1901."

Properly instructed by conductor Dodge, I jumped ahead a year to the issue for January 1901. There I found a lead article titled "The Dawn of the Twentieth Century" by a writer named Tudor Jenks. "Days, weeks, months, and years pass without especial wonder," Jenks wrote. "But the ending of a century comes but once to almost all of us, and history gives to each hundred years a character of its own."

Jenks then went on to recount (briefly) what had happened in each century, from the first through the nineteenth. Near the end of the piece, he summed up the story thus far: "The steam-engine has brought the whole world within reach of every nation; the telegraph brings all happenings within knowledge; modern weapons have made the most advanced nations irresistible by untrained peoples; the printing-press brings the intelligence of whole peoples to bear on every question. Electricity becomes man's servant, and he learns to turn forces into one another."

Jenks made no predictions, however, about what was likely to happen in the century ahead. If he had, he would almost certainly have mentioned some of the topics—from politics to transportation to the changing role of women—that are explored in the pages of this anthology. He might even have begun, as this book does, with an evaluation of the science fiction writings of two of his contemporaries, Jules Verne and H. G. Wells. But it's not likely Jenks would have composed as provocative and enlightening a piece as the one contributed to this volume by Russell Freedman.

The Century That Was does not pretend to be a comprehensive chronicle of everything significant that happened in the twentieth century. There is no discussion, for instance, of the phenomenal growth and development of the movies, starting with the silent, flickering, black-and-white shorts that were projected in storefront "nickelodeons," and culminating in the special effects–filled blockbusters that are shown in mall cineplexes today.

Nor is there an account of the vast changes that took place in the way Americans obtained news of what was going on in the world. At the beginning of the century, such information came almost entirely via the written word in newspapers and magazines. By the late 1920s, radio broadcasts and movie newsreels had been added to the media mix. They, in turn, were followed by television after World War II and by the Internet in the last years of the century. As these changes occurred, the means by which most information was conveyed shifted dramatically from the verbal to the visual.

Instead of a comprehensive report, this book offers a selection of topics that the individual contributors were eager to explore. Each writer was encouraged to approach his or her subject in whatever way seemed most comfortable and appropriate. The result is a lively, stimulating, and sometimes quirky gathering of essays, no two of which are alike in terms of voice or style.

Several of the pieces are marvels of distillation, managing to depict a century of activity in a small number of pages. Notable among these are Milton Meltzer's clear-eyed survey of American politics from the presidency of Theodore Roosevelt to that of Bill Clinton; Penny Colman's entertaining and informative account of the progress American women made on various fronts; Laurence Pringle's compelling summary of the conservation movement and the campaign to protect the environment; and Walter Dean Myers's panoramic overview of the civil rights struggle, highlighted by contrasting biographical sketches of Martin Luther King, Jr. and Malcolm X.

Other essays focus closely on a single event or development that affected American life in some major way. Examples of this approach can be found in Jim Murphy's revealing investigation of the myriad changes brought about by the automobile; in Bruce Brooks's unsettling portrayal of the shift in emphasis in sports from the amateur to the professional; and in Albert Marrin's in-depth study of the long-term effects of America's participation in World War I.

Still others assume a refreshingly personal stance. Eve Bunting frames her essay on immigration with poignant memories of her own experiences when she, her husband, and their three young children emigrated to America from Northern Ireland. Through a skillful blending of words and family photos, Lois Lowry traces the ins and outs of fashion as they were reflected in the lives of six generations of women in her family. Katherine Paterson compares her beliefs with those of her minister father as she meditates on the status of religion in twentieth-century America and the often heated conflict that developed between religion and science.

It's interesting to note how many of the essays connect and interrelate. For example, Milton Meltzer's political history incorporates aspects of the civil rights movement and the fight for women's rights. By the same token, Penny Colman's essay on women is in part a political history, as are Walter Dean Myers's account of the civil rights movement, Katherine Paterson's thoughts on religion, and Eve Bunting's survey of immigration. Albert Marrin's chronicle of World War I overlaps with the struggle for greater equality of both women and blacks.

All of the essays look ahead in one way or another toward the twenty-first century. Several emphasize the important role young people can play in advancing worthy causes. Milton Meltzer mentions the more than one hundred million Americans, eight million of them between the ages of fourteen and seventeen, who volunteer their time each week in various community activities. Laurence Pringle describes the accomplishments of young people across the country who have taken part in the fight to preserve the environment. "They knew," he writes, "that the twenty-first century would bring new problems, new challenges."

In this, young people today are not so different from the young people who greeted the arrival of the last century. They, too, looked forward to a new era filled with challenges and opportunities. One of them, Marguerite Knopf, age seventeen, expressed her feelings in a poem that appeared in *St. Nicholas*. Here are the concluding stanzas of Marguerite's poem, which could have been written yesterday:

> *Good-by, old dying century;*
> *We welcome in the new;*
> *And in the next one hundred years*
> *Let's see what man can do.*
>
> *The generation coming—*
> *And that is you and I—*
> *Will be the men and women*
> *To whom the nations cry.*
>
> *Oh, welcome to the century!*
> *The chances that it brings*
> *For you and me to fill the world*
> *With grand and joyous things!*

RUSSELL FREEDMAN

LOOKING BACK
AT LOOKING FORWARD:
Predicting the Twentieth Century

In the coming century, engineers will control the climate by flicking a switch and turning a dial. Deserts will be transformed into gardens, the polar ice caps will be melted, and the entire earth will enjoy perpetual spring.

Cities in the next century will have skyscrapers a thousand feet tall, boulevards a hundred yards wide, and moving sidewalks for pedestrians. Homes throughout the world will be linked by televised telephones. Trains will speed through pneumatic tubes at a thousand miles an hour, luxury airliners will fly nonstop to any point on earth, and manned spaceships will race off to planets circling distant suns.

The *next* century? Those predictions were made more than a hundred years ago by the French author Jules Verne, who peered through a keyhole of the future into our own twentieth century with surprising accuracy. As far back as 1865, when passenger-carrying balloons were the most advanced form of aircraft, Verne wrote about a trip to the moon in a rocket-equipped projectile. His story was so convincing that hundreds of people volunteered to ride in the spaceship he had "invented."

While some of Verne's predictions have yet to be realized, many others that seemed fantastic at the time are now established fact. He sent his heroes to the North Pole forty-five years before Robert E. Peary, to the South Pole forty-one years before Roald Amudsen. In an era when city streets were illuminated by gas lamps, he foresaw the widespread use of electricity in everyday life. When oceangoing ships still carried sails, he envisioned an around-the-world voyage in an all-electric submarine. He described airplanes and helicopters when the Wright brothers were still building bicycles. And he wrote about television newscasts before Guglielmo Marconi had even thought of the wireless telegraph.

Verne predicted motion pictures, wirephotos, color photography, recorded books, air conditioners, computers, synthetic materials, condensed foods, prefabricated mass housing, public health programs, air pollution control, and space satellites before any of those things actually existed. He also prophesied guided missiles that could annihilate cities, lethal fallout that could make large areas uninhabitable, and the modern totalitarian state, with its secret police and enforced regimentation.

Verne did not originate what we now call "science fiction." Stories about amazing inventions, discoveries, and journeys go all the way back to ancient times, yet those early tales were usually based more on fantasy than on fact. Verne was the first author to write an entire series of stories dramatizing the scientific and technological accomplishments of an era and predicting the future outcome of those accomplishments. He popularized such stories and established them as a special branch of fiction. For those reasons, he is usually considered the founder of modern science fiction.

When he first started writing his series of "Extraordinary Journeys" during the 1860s, the achievements of explorers, inventors, and scientists were inspiring widespread popular interest in those regions of the earth that were still unmapped and in the powers of science and technology to change people's lives. Verne's novels focusing on these developments became wildly popular. His books were translated into dozens of languages. They were read not only by the young people for whom they were originally intended, but by enthusiastic readers of all ages and in every walk of life. Verne's name became a household word in France and in places like Russia and the United States, where some of his stories take place and where many of the accomplishments he envisioned would, in fact, be realized.

One of Verne's devoted fans was a British youngster named Herbert George Wells, who grew up during the 1870s when Verne was writing some of his best-known stories. During the 1890s, Wells took his place beside the French author as another master of science fiction. Like Verne, he sent his heroes from the earth to the moon. And he predicted many scientific and technological developments, such as television, intercontinental airplanes, air-conditioned cities, and nuclear warfare.

Wells was the first author to write about a time machine, an "invention" that could carry its operator to any point in the future or the past. His short novel *The Time Machine* (1895) describes an imaginary world in the distant future. And he was the first to imagine an invasion of the earth by aliens from another planet. *The War of the Worlds* (1898) describes with hair-raising realism how Martians—superior beings with super advanced technology—land in England and lay waste to turn-of-the-century London.

Forty years after its publication, the novel was dramatized on the radio by Orson Welles, who changed the setting to New Jersey and presented the story in the form of news flashes and on-the-scene interviews. Welles's broadcast seemed so nightmarishly real that hundreds of listeners panicked and fled into the countryside, seeking places to hide from the invading Martians.

H. G. Wells was often called the "English Jules Verne," a term that made him furious. While he had read Verne's books avidly as a boy, he insisted that there was a world of difference between himself and the French writer. Verne emphatically agreed. Neither man regarded himself as the French or English equivalent of the other.

Verne's aim was to convey scientific and technological information by means of an exciting story. He narrated his heroes' adventures with documentary precision, describing in minute detail the methods they

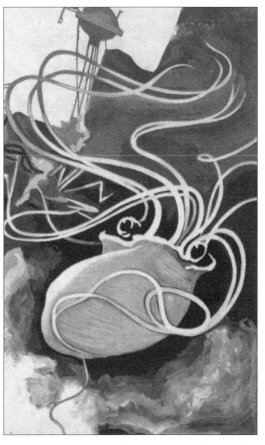

Creature from Mars. (From *The War of the Worlds* by H. G. Wells)

use and the conditions they encounter. Wells, in contrast, gave his imagination a much wider latitude and was not so scrupulous about the factual basis of his stories.

Verne's work dealt with the actual possibilities of invention and discovery. "He wrote and believed and told that this thing or that could be done, which was not at that time done," said Wells in his introduction to his own *Collected Scientific Romances*. "He helped his readers to imagine it done and to realize what fun, excitement, or mischief might ensue. Many of his inventions have 'come true.' But these stories of mine collected here do not pretend to deal with possible things; they are exercises of the imagination in a quite different field."

Verne aimed for absolute realism. He tried to avoid saying anything in his stories that could not be justified by the science of the time. He crammed his stories with technical explanations that made it easier for the reader to accept his imaginative plots. A tale about a trip to the moon was filled with the same attention to detail as a story about a train trip from Paris to Marseilles.

Wells, on the other hand, was less interested in strict scientific realism than in exploring the effects of science and technology on human behavior. He disposed of the scientific machinery and gadgetry quickly in his books, asking the reader to suspend disbelief, if only for a moment, so that he could get on with his story.

In *The Time Machine,* Wells does not offer any explanation of how that machine functions or the manner in which his hero, the Time Traveller, managed to build it. His science fiction tales are not so much about the advance of science as about the reaction of human beings to that advance. *The Time Machine* gave Wells an opportunity to imagine the future evolution of the human race, while *The War of the Worlds* allowed him to speculate on the behavior of humans in the face of utter catastrophe.

After publishing several "scientific romances," as he called his science fiction, Wells turned from the fantastic to the realistic. He began to write satirical novels about contemporary British life, social and political commentary, and, later, popularized accounts of history and science. Verne also wrote popular history, but he remained primarily a writer of science fiction and a prophet of the future until his death in 1905.

Jules Verne wasn't the first writer to imagine a trip to the moon. The oldest known tale about a moon journey, called *True History,* was written about A.D. 160 by the Greek satirist Lucian of Samosata, who tells how a sailing ship is carried up to the moon by a whirlwind. In 1683, Francis Godwin, the distinguished bishop of Hereford in England, wrote *The Man in the Moon,* a hugely popular story, translated into many languages, in which the hero travels to the moon on a platform pulled by trained birds. And in *Comic History of the States and Empires of the Moon* (1656), by the French wit and adventurer Cyrano de Bergerac, the hero takes off for the moon in a flying chariot powered by fireworks, or rockets.

There were dozens of stories like these, most of them intended to be humorous. When they were written, little was known about interplanetary space. No one had the vaguest idea how a real space journey might be accomplished. In a typical story, the hero devises some fantastic method of reaching the moon, and once he arrives, he discovers a satirical version of life on earth.

The American writer Edgar Allan Poe joined this tradition in 1835 when he wrote *The Unparalleled Adventure of One Hans Pfaal,* a whimsical tale about a Dutchman who flies to the moon in a giant balloon. By then, scientists had learned quite a bit about conditions in space, so Poe had to be more careful than his predecessors. He describes in vivid detail the killing effects of high altitudes on a flying man. Hans Pfaal suffers terribly from cold and lack of air before he finally encloses his balloon-car in an airtight envelope, which carries its own supply of oxygen. This was the first "space capsule" ever described in fiction.

Poe claimed that his story was different from earlier imaginary moon journeys because he had applied "scientific principles to the actual passage between the earth and the moon." However, he abandoned those principles when he tried to convince his readers that a thin atmosphere extends from the earth to the moon. Without such an atmosphere, Poe could not hope to send his balloon into space. Since a balloon is buoyed up by the surrounding atmosphere, it can't fly without air. When *Hans Pfaal* was written, scientists knew (and Poe undoubtedly knew) that interplanetary space is an airless vacuum. So Hans Pfaal's trip to the moon was just as fantastic as the journeys made by earlier fictional moon travelers.

Thirty years later, when Jules Verne wrote *From the Earth to the Moon* (1865), he wanted to tell a story that would rely solely on the knowledge, techniques, and materials available at that time. Passenger-carrying balloons were still the latest word in air travel. No airplane had ever left the ground. The steam engine was the only practical man-made source of mechanical energy, and since steam engines require air for combustion, they cannot function in space.

Verne understood that a real space vehicle must be able to escape the earth's gravitational pull, function in airless space, and speed across the vast distances separating the earth from the moon and the planets. It must supply its passengers with a life-sustaining artificial atmosphere and protect them from the many hazards of a space journey.

Verne took all of these factors into account. He decided to send a projectile to the moon by firing it from a nine-hundred-foot-long cannon at an initial velocity of seven miles per second (what we now call "escape velocity")—fast enough to escape the earth's gravitational pull and continue moving out into space. The projectile is made of aluminum, which had been prepared in its pure form for the first time in 1854 and was still a rare and expensive metal. Inside the bullet-shaped projectile is an airtight passenger compartment equipped with a chemical device that produces a steady supply of oxygen.

Verne's three astronauts take along plenty of water and concentrated food, scientific instruments, tools, weapons, maps of the moon, and seeds for possible planting on the moon. For protection, the walls of the projectile are heavily insulated. The base is outfitted with water buffers and with powerful steel springs designed to protect the passengers from the tremendous concussion that will occur when the cannon is fired.

Launching the projectile from a 900-foot-long cannon sunk in the ground. (From *From the Earth to the Moon* by Jules Verne)

Finally, several small rockets of the kind used in fireworks displays are attached to the outside of the projectile. Verne had done his homework. He explains that a rocket can fire in airless space. As his travelers approach their destination and start falling toward the moon, pulled by lunar gravity, they intend to fire their rockets in order to slow their descent and make a "soft" landing on the moon.

The story takes place in the United States, where the mammoth cannon is built by members of a gun club as "a grand experiment worthy of the nineteenth century." The launching site is on the coast of Florida. And while the launch itself is successful, the projectile is deflected from its intended course when it almost collides with a great meteoroid. Instead of landing on the moon, it is swept into orbit around the moon. It becomes an artificial satellite. And that is where the story ends.

Soon after the publication of *From the Earth to the Moon,* the eagerly awaited sequel, *All Around the Moon,* began to appear as installments in a popular French magazine before its publication as a book in 1870. As the astronauts travel in orbit, they study the moon's surface with their binoculars and telescopes. Verne carefully confined his description of the lunar surface to the known facts about the moon at that time. His astronauts see nothing that had not already been seen through earthbound telescopes. Below them lies a stark landscape of jagged mountains, bowl-shaped craters, and barren plateaus. There are no signs of water, atmosphere, or life.

Finally, they fire their rockets in an attempt to land on the lunar surface as originally planned. Instead, as their projectile is thrown out of orbit, it starts to fall back toward the earth, heading to a safe splashdown in the Pacific Ocean—precisely the fail-safe program of the Apollo mission a century later and almost exactly the flight path of the damaged *Apollo 13* in April 1970.

In these two novels, Verne correctly predicted several features of modern space travel. He foresaw that a space capsule would become white-hot as it raced through the earth's atmosphere, that its

Firing rockets to knock the projectile out of orbit. (From *All Around the Moon* by Jules Verne)

passengers would experience weightlessness, and that its course could be changed by firing rockets. He was the first writer to describe an artificial satellite in orbit. And he recognized the basic principle involved in reaching the moon: If an object attains sufficient velocity in the right direction at the right time, it will escape the earth's gravitational pull, enter the moon's gravitational field, and start falling toward the moon.

All of the calculations and mathematical equations governing the moon shot are presented as part of the story. While much of this technical data was baffling to ordinary readers, its inclusion suggested that Verne was describing a scientifically feasible project. Scientists who read the books were aware of serious practical objections to Verne's moon shot. For one thing, if a projectile were actually shot out of a cannon at a velocity of seven miles per second, the passengers would be killed instantly by the sudden acceleration.

Even so, many readers were convinced that the novels were an accurate prediction of things to come. Some readers believed that Verne was writing about a spaceship that did, in fact, exist and that a real trip to the moon was imminent. Verne received hundreds of letters from volunteers—men and women alike—who wanted to go along on the first trip to the moon. "The Parisians are certainly brave," he wrote to his brother. "Some of them are determined by hook or crook to embark on my projectile."

A generation later, when H. G. Wells wrote *The First Men in the Moon* (1901), the last of his scientific romances, he had an entirely different type of story in mind. Unlike Verne, he wasted little time describing his spaceship. He simply borrowed a device used by some earlier writers: his hero invented "Cavorite," a substance that could eliminate the force of gravity. Verne, who was then seventy-three, rather huffily pointed out that cannons and rockets are real objects familiar to everyone, while a gravity-insulating metal is pure fantasy, a figment of the imagination. "I sent my travelers to the moon with gunpowder," he said, "a thing one may see every day. Where does Monsieur Wells find his Cavorite? Let him show it to me!"

Wells was less interested in *how* his travelers reached the moon than in what happened after they arrived. The world they found was nothing at all like the one described by Jules Verne. Wells's moon had just enough water and atmosphere to support life. Beneath the lunar surface, his travelers discover an eerie world inhabited by creatures with giant antlike bodies and superhuman brains. Through the use of science and technology, they have mastered their harsh environment and created a highly developed but nightmarish society ruled by the Grand Lunar, who has a stunted body "with insect-jointed limbs shriveled and white" and a massive brain that radiates a brilliant, blinding light, "a brain very much like an opaque, featureless bladder, with dim, undulating ghosts of convolutions writing visibly within."

Wells knew that the moon is a hopelessly dead world. And he knew that there is no such thing as an antigravity substance. Yet he was not trying to present a realistic account of a trip to the moon. His imaginary lunar world is a dramatic device that allows him to satirize human life on earth and to comment on his generation's smug confidence in the ability of science and technology to solve all problems.

Verne eventually wrote sixty-three Extraordinary Journeys, sending his heroes to virtually every unexplored region on earth. In *The Adventures of Captain Hatteras* (1866), Hatteras and his companions make their way to the North Pole by dogsled and discover that the Pole is located at the summit of a flaming volcano. Here, Verne guessed wrong, of course, since the North Pole is actually located in the midst of the permanent ice cap that covers much of the Arctic Ocean. However, Verne was writing nearly half a century before Robert E. Peary reached the Pole for the first time in 1909.

In *Twenty Thousand Leagues Under the Sea* (1870), Verne sent his imaginary submarine *Nautilus* sailing beneath the polar ice cap toward the South Pole, which was first reached in real life by the Norweigian explorer Roald Amundsen in 1911. The secret of the *Nautilus* is electricity. When Verne wrote this novel, electricity was still in the experimental stage. Scientists and engineers had not yet developed electric motors and generators powerful enough for practical use.

Moon creatures. (From *The First Men in the Moon* by H. G. Wells)

Even so, the *Nautilus* is an electrical marvel. Electricity produced by powerful batteries turns the submarine's propellers and provides heat and light for the vessel. Electric pumps circulate fresh air throughout the craft. Electricity is used to evaporate seawater and make it drinkable. All the ship's cooking is done by electricity. And as an added touch, the steel hull of the *Nautilus* can be charged with electricity to fend off unwanted intruders. All this when Thomas Edison's lightbulb was still several years in the future.

Commanded by the mysterious genius Captain Nemo, the *Nautilus* sails the oceans of the world, plunging into the depths of storm-tossed seas and cruising smoothly along the ocean floor at a speed of fifty miles per hour. When the first real oceangoing submarines were introduced at the end of the nineteenth century, they bore some striking resemblances to Verne's visionary *Nautilus*. Escape hatches, ballast tanks, horizontal rudders, air-conditioning systems, electric instruments—generally similar to those described by Verne—all became part of modern submarines. Electric storage batteries, used to supply the power for underwater cruising, were standard submarine equipment until the advent of today's nuclear-powered submarines. Verne would have been pleased to know that the first atomic submarine, launched in 1954, was named the USS *Nautilus*.

Verne was seventeen years ahead of the Wright brothers' first successful flight when he wrote about a heavier-than-air flying machine in *Robur the Conqueror* (also known as *Clipper of the Clouds*), published in 1886. Robur's *Albatross* resembles an oceangoing liner sailing through the clouds. The aircraft is built of specially treated compressed paper, which forms "a material as hard as steel . . . and far lighter."

Rising from the deck of the *Albatross* are thirty-seven masts, each holding two horizontal propellers—the *Albatross* is a helicopter. Its seventy-four horizontal propellers lift it into the air. Two large vertical propellers, one at the bow and the other at the stern, propel the craft through the air at the incredible speed of one hundred and twenty miles per hour: "This speed is that of the storm which tears up trees by the roots. It is the speed of the carrier pigeon, and is only surpassed by the flight of the swallow and that of the swift. In a word, the

Albatross, by using the whole force of her propellers, could fly around the world in two hundred hours, or less than eight days."

Like Captain Nemo before him, Robur runs his ship on electricity. The electric storage batteries on the *Albatross* can furnish power for six months before being recharged. Also like Nemo, Robur is a fiercely independent man who distrusts organized society. As the novel ends, he declares that he dare not give up the secret of his flying machine. "I know that people's minds are not yet ready for that important revolution which the conquest of the air will one day bring," he says. "I go then, and I take my secret with me. But it will not be lost to humanity. It will belong to you the day you are ready to profit from it, and wise enough not to abuse it."

The power of electricity to transform the world is a recurring theme in a number of Verne's novels, stories, and articles. Writing for an American magazine called the *Forum* in 1889, he predicted that industry, transportation, and communication would depend in the future on electrical power derived from rivers and waterfalls, from winds and tides, from the interior of the earth, and from the rays of the sun. Machines called "accumulators" would control the climate by storing up the summer's heat and releasing it into the atmosphere during the winter. Every home would be equipped with a "phono-telephote set," combining the principles of the telephone and television. Printed newspapers would be obsolete; the news would be heard and seen instead through the telephote screen. Businesses would rely on automatic computers, by which "the most complex calculations can be made in a few seconds."

When Verne made these predictions, telephones, electric lights, and electric power were still novelties, but they were being developed rapidly. During the 1880s, the first telephone exchanges appeared in a few large cities; gas lamps were just beginning to give way to electric lighting; and industry still depended on steam for mechanical power. Practical television and computers were still decades in the future.

For the most part, Verne's early novels and stories are optimistic about the future. His heroes use their knowledge, skills, and inventions for the benefit of humanity. As Verne grew older, however, he became increasingly concerned about the dangerous misuse of science and technology. In one of his most disturbingly prophetic novels, *The Begum's Fortune* (1879), he envisioned enlightened town planning, the modern totalitarian state, and the era of total destruction.

The novel tells the story of two scientists who jointly inherit the fortune of a princess from India; each man uses his half of the fortune to build a city, expressing his ideals and aspirations, in a remote region of southern Oregon.

Dr. Sarrasin builds Frankville, "a model city based on strictly scientific principles," where scientific knowledge is used for humanity's benefit. Frankville occupies a beautiful site overlooking the Pacific. A sunny technological utopia, it has broad, tree-lined streets, fine parks and gardens, impressive public buildings, and plenty of space, light, and air.

In dramatic contrast to Frankville is Stahlstadt, or City of Steel, built by Professor Schultz. Located on an arid mountain plateau, the city is an ugly industrial complex where the noise of machinery is heard constantly and where "the air is heavy with smoke, which hangs like a pall over the ground. Not a bird nor an insect is to be found, and a butterfly has not been seen within the memory of man."

Stahlstadt is devoted to the manufacture of weapons, which Professor Schultz sells, at a fat profit, to anyone who can afford them. Since he intends to guard his manufacturing secrets from prying eyes, his city is a grim dictatorship, complete with a secret police force, where technology is applied to the suppression of freedom. In Stahlstadt, human values have been sacrificed to ruthless industrial efficiency. The city's workers are scarcely regarded as human beings. They are numbers, replaceable units in the mass-production process. Instead of being liberated by machines, they have been enslaved by them.

Professor Schultz has invented a superweapon, a long-range cannon that fires a projectile "charged with liquid carbonic acid" under extreme pressure. When the projectile explodes, "an enormous volume of carbonic acid will rush into the air, and a cold of a hundred degrees below zero will seize upon the surrounding atmosphere." Every living creature will be frozen to death on the spot. The projectile also has a lingering fallout effect, since the gas remains "a very long time near the ground."

Thus, Verne imagined a weapon even more efficient than today's nuclear bombs, for Schultz's projectile can kill without destroying property. "With my plan," boasts Schultz, "there will be no wounded, only dead!"

In the end, the evil professor foils himself when he accidentally drops a glass vial containing a few drops of his lethal gas. He is frozen to death instantly in his laboratory. Verne concludes the novel with the hope that "the example of Frankville and Stahlstadt, as model city and industrial town, will not be lost upon future generations."

When Jules Verne died at his home in Amiens, France, in 1905, at the age of seventy-seven, the world was fast catching up with many of his visions. He foresaw the possibility of a glorious future, when scientists would use their knowledge to create a technological utopia for all humanity. But he also came to realize that scientific advances do not necessarily lead to social progress, and he was haunted by the possibility that humanity would fail to use its growing powers wisely.

Verne never reconciled his faith in the blessings of science and his fear of its perils. That conflict between optimism and dread as he peered into the future has proven to be his most prophetic vision— a vision he shared with H. G. Wells. Both writers predicted that the "science of the future" would create marvelous machines and conquer the forces of nature. And both men warned that science and

Professor Schultz and his superweapon. (From *The Begum's Fortune* by Jules Verne)

technology, if abused, could become a Frankenstein monster, resulting in weapons of mass destruction, in debasement of the earth's environment, and in the suppression of human freedom and dignity.

Today, as we enter a new millennium, those warnings seem as timely as ever—even more timely, in fact, than in the science fiction tales of H. G. Wells and Jules Verne.

———

Russell Freedman is the author of more than forty books on subjects ranging from animal behavior to American history. He was awarded the Newbery Medal for his book *Lincoln: A Photobiography,* and Newbery Honors for *The Wright Brothers: How They Invented the Airplane* and *Eleanor Roosevelt: A Life of Discovery*. In 1998, Mr. Freedman received the Laura Ingalls Wilder Award, in recognition of his body of work. He lives in New York City but travels widely to gather material for his books.

IMMIGRANTS ALL

My heart was breaking. "I don't want to go," I whispered. And right at that moment, I didn't want to.

My husband, my three small children, and I were boarding a plane in Ireland to start a new life in California, USA.

The decision to leave had been wrenching. It has been said that the urge to emigrate is born out of either "push" or "pull." "Push," because for some reason—economic or political perhaps—you need to go. "Pull" because you have relatives already in the far country, and the tug is strong to go where they are, where the grass is greener and the sun shines brighter. Whichever way and for whatever reason, it is never easy.

For us, the push was to make a better future for ourselves and our children. Northern Ireland, where even then in 1959 the threat of "the Troubles" loomed large and dark, was not a good place to raise a family. My ambitious husband had gone as far as he could in the Irish workplace. So the determination was made.

We came on a DC-6B, a comparatively small plane, because back then there were no passenger jets flying. The trip seemed to take forever. Perhaps forever is a good way to make the transition between the old world and the new, the familiar life and the untried one. Our journey took twenty-two hours, over the polar ice cap. We landed to refuel in the Arctic, and all of it seemed like a dream, and not a happy one. I tried not to think of the grandparents left behind, waving as our plane lifted. Crying.

Oh, it was hard.

It is always hard.

In 1831, Rebecca Burlend, coming to America with her family to farm, wrote about her thoughts:

It was at Liverpool . . . that the throes of leaving England and all its endearments put our courage to a test. . . . We sat in profound silence for an hour together. Only now and then a sigh would escape us. . . . I not unfrequently observed [my dear husband's] eyes suffused with tears, which though unnoticed by him,

Irish emigrants leaving their home for America. (Library of Congress)

fell . . . down his sunbrowned cheeks. . . . "O Rebecca, I cannot do it, I cannot do it!"

But they did it, as so many before them had done and as so many after them would do. I hope Rebecca and her "dear husband" found fulfillment.

To understand immigration in the twentieth century, it helps to go back to the beginnings. In the early days of the colonies, immigrants were warmly invited. In Northern Ireland, it was reported that agents, paid by ships' captains, wandered the markets and fairs enticing people with tales of fine acreage in America, "and no taxes or tithes to be paid either."

Leaflets were handed out describing this land of milk and honey. For those who couldn't afford the price of passage, arrangements could be made, they said. Perhaps they would be willing to sign papers promising that they would work as indentured servants on plantations in return for the money to get to the New World. They would be given food, clothing, and shelter. What a deal, and for only seven years of indentured servitude.

There were so many takers that, in 1619, John Pory of Virginia wrote: "Our principall wealth consisteth in Servants."

A ship's captain could "buy" an indentured servant in Europe and sell him in America. Eighty-four dollars was considered a suitable price and gave the captain a good profit over and above the cost of bringing the man. Sometimes he did not come voluntarily. A young man might be picked up off the streets, kidnapped, and drugged. He would wake up aboard a heaving, lurching ship, not knowing how he happened to be there or where he was going. Many a mother searched and mourned for her lost son, never to be heard from again.

Before landing, the servants-to-be were cleaned up, given haircuts, sometimes adorned with wigs to make them more attractive before they were sold. As soon as the ship docked, they were lined up on the deck so the planters, anxious to buy, could come on board and look them over. They would check their teeth, feel their muscles, and bid for them at auction.

Often the ships carried no other cargo but servants, who might be driven to town like cattle to be sold off. "Soul drivers" the sellers were called. "Body sellers," too. Some of those who came to work as servants were convicts, sent by English lawmakers to the colonies to serve out their terms by laboring. It is doubtful which was better—hard labor at home or hard labor for a new master.

> Five years served I under Master Guy,
> In the land of Virginny, O,
> Which made me for to know
> Sorrow, grief and woe,
> when I was weary, weary, O.

The difference between this trade and the trade in African slaves was that after his time was up, the indentured servant was free, the slave never. Or not until emancipation or death. The servant might have learned a trade while "owned," and he could put it to use later. But many died before their time was up or were never able to make it on their

Inspection and sale of a Negro. (Schomburg Center, New York Public Library)

own. Twenty percent did beat the odds and became landowners themselves or overseers on plantations. Did *they* use indentured servants? Did they remember how it had been for them, and were they kind?

The women who came under the same programs usually fared better than the men. Women were much in demand as brides in a country where females were scarce. Women who started out cleaning house or milking cows might end up as mistresses of their own homes.

For the slaves, there were few happy endings.

It's impossible to imagine the terror of the African, taken in shackles from his home and put on a ship to cross the ocean in the most inhuman and horrible manner possible. Then, when he landed, he found himself purchased by a master who owned him for life.

ADVERTISEMENT
To be sold on board the ship Bance-Island,
on Tuesday the 6th of May next, at Ashley-Ferry;
a choice cargo of about 250 fine healthy negroes,
just arrived from the Windward and Rice Coast.

Approximately two hundred thousand black slaves were brought to America during the eighteenth century, many of them destined to work on plantations in the southern states. One slave wrote that those fields to be tilled seemed to stretch "from one end of the earth to the other." Although escape was difficult, many slaves tried to run away. The Underground Railway, an escape route run by sympathetic free blacks and whites, helped thousands get to the North. But the majority lived their lives in bondage. In despair they sang their "sorrow songs," hoping for a better life, if not in this world then in the next.

> *I'm just a poor wayfarin' stranger,*
> *A-traveling through this world of woe;*
> *But there's no sickness, toil, or danger*
> *In that bright world to which I go.*

The slave trade was forced immigration at its worst and was one of

Invitation to an unsurpassed farming region in southern Minnesota and Eastern Dakota. (Minnesota Historical Society)

the main factors that led to the Civil War. It is still a blot on America's conscience. To hear a Negro spiritual sung today is to feel the pain and think of a time that is thankfully behind us.

At the end of the Civil War, the slaves were freed, and in the late years of the nineteenth century and the early part of the twentieth, immigration from abroad was encouraged.

"The bosom of America is open . . . to the oppressed and persecuted of all Nations and Religions,"George Washington had said.

There were vast western acres waiting to be settled. There were vacant lands waiting to be sold. Posters across Europe announced: "Emigrants look to your interest. Farms at $3 an acre and not a foot of it waste land."

The railroads had only recently linked the East and the West. Now they hoped to increase their business by encouraging the immigrants in every way they could. Some railroad companies built places for eating and sleeping along the routes. There were churches at some stops and even schools. Thousands of pamphlets were distributed in western Europe inviting emigrants to try living in Missouri, Kansas, Minnesota, Iowa. The emigrants came and they tried.

For some, the dream of a new life turned into a nightmare. Distrust and resentment of the newcomers developed, particularly of those who settled in the cities. They were different. They looked different, spoke a different language, and, worst of all, they took jobs away from "true Americans."

The poor and unemployed immigrants were forced to settle in the slums and sometimes fell into lives of crime. They were seen as dirty, thieving, lazy. Looking desperately for work, the immigrants read advertisements that said: "Wanted . . . a cook or a chambermaid. They must be American, Scotch, Swiss, or Africans. No Irish need apply." Interesting that by then, people of African descent were more acceptable than some other applicants.

A popular song of the time, sung by the Irish, tried to put a humorous slant on the frustration of looking for jobs that were denied to them from the start:

Emigrants coming to America.
(Museum of the City of New York)

I'm a decent boy just landed from
the town of Ballyfad;
I want a situation and I want it very bad.
I've seen employment advertised, "It's just the thing," say I,
But the dirty spalpeen [rascal] ended with "No Irish need apply."

In the last verse, Pat, "the decent boy," gives the would-be employer a good walloping and tells him good-bye with this advice: "When next you want a beating write 'No Irish need apply.'"

But the song was only a song and changed nothing.

There was also a deep fear in America of the Chinese, often called "The Yellow Peril," whose labor was cheap and who worked hard for the little they got.

Thousands of Chinese came looking for wealth in the gold fields of California. They scraped together passage money for the three-month trip to the country they called *Gum Shan,* "Mountain of Gold."

Crocker's Pets: Chinese immigrants.
(California Historical Society)

"The Chinese must go" was the rallying cry of western politicians who knew their constituents felt threatened by the Chinese immigrants. "Anti-coolie" clubs sprang up. WE EMPLOY NOT CHINESE LABOR HERE read the signs. Rather strange grammatically but to the point.

In 1882, the Chinese Exclusion Act was passed. This law shut off all future immigration from China except for teachers, diplomats, and merchants. Forgotten were the welcoming words of George Washington. That old fear of emigrants taking jobs from "true Americans" worked against the Chinese laborer— though it is doubtful how many "true Americans" would have wanted to work as hard as the Chinese coolies did. Like the Irish, they had helped to build the railroads.

Charles Crocker, the construction boss of the Canadian Pacific Railway, had been the first to see the potential of using cheap Chinese workers to lay track. He brought fifty of them from Sacramento's Chinatown and hired them to work on his railroad. They were so industrious and so undemanding that he sent word to China saying he would hire two thousand more if they came. Thousands did, jammed into boats in conditions worse than those for livestock. Many of us think of boats as pleasure craft. It is extraordinary how often, for the immigrant, they were the first warnings of horrors to come.

"Crocker's Pets," as the Chinese were called, worked on the transcontinental railway, slicing its way through the High Sierra. The work was so dangerous that a thousand died, hanging in baskets over sheer cliffs as they placed charges of dynamite, laboring beyond exhaustion. As fast as the Chinese died, they were replaced. The ships that brought the new workers from China took the dead back to be buried in their homeland. Despised, rejected, tormented, especially by their Irish coworkers, the Chinese lived lives of despair with few rights other than the right to lay those tracks. A white could shoot a Chinese without fear of punishment. The life of a Chinese immigrant was thought to be without value.

Immigrants from other lands poured in. They came from Europe, Asia, the world over. Many came, as we did, from Ireland, laborers whose sweat helped build the Erie Canal and whose muscle laid most of the railroad track that ran eventually from New York to St. Louis.

In eighteen hundred and forty-two
I left the Old World for the New.
Bad cess to the luck that brought me through
to work upon the railway,

Pat sang, pounding the ties and hefting the steel. It has been said that America was built by horsepower, steam power, and Irish power. It has also been said that in the 1830s, when Pat arrived in America, not only were the streets not paved with gold, they were not paved at all—and he was expected to pave them.

Many immigrants came from Germany, sturdy, strong men and women unafraid to travel the Oregon Trail, doing their part to open the way west. Others came from Sweden and the Netherlands, all of them bringing their skills and their honesty and their work ethic.

The Germans also brought with them their love of music, their traditions, their memories. One memory was of the Christmas song, "Stille Nacht," which became "Silent Night," the classic carol of Christmas. It was the Germans, too, who gave us the tradition of the Christmas tree.

The wave of immigrants only increased as America entered the twentieth century. They came from Italy, four million of them by 1920, and from Russia, many of them Jews escaping anti-Semitism. The Jews carried with them their rich culture, their religious beliefs, and Yiddish, their mother tongue.

These were willing immigrants who would strengthen the backbone of the nation. The majority arrived in the port of New York. For those who came after 1886, the Statue of Liberty was the first symbol of America they saw.

I know their feeling of awe, though not to the emotional extent that those immigrants knew it. As a young girl, many years before my own family emigrated, I sailed with my mother to New York from Ireland. We came to visit my mother's brother, himself an immigrant who had left Ireland in poverty in the 1920s. He was doing well . . . "our rich Yankee" we called him.

There was great excitement aboard our ship the night before we were scheduled to sail into New York Harbor. Every single passenger was up on deck at 3:00 A.M., huddled cold along the railings, straining for a first glimpse of the famous Lady, holding high the torch of liberty.

She appeared suddenly out of the mysterious dark, a mythical figure, gigantic, powerful, and there wasn't a sound from those watching as we glided silently past the statue. I remember that my mother cried, and seeing her tears, I wept, too, though I wasn't sure why.

Now I imagine those earlier immigrants crowding the decks of their ships, stunned by the knowledge that they were here. They'd made it.

A poem about the statue, written by Emma Lazarus in 1883, has come to mean hope for the oppressed of the world. The words are printed on a large plaque that is now in the Statue of Liberty museum.

"Give me your tired, your poor, your huddled masses yearning to breathe free," the Statue of Liberty commanded. And they, tired and poor and yearning to breathe free, were here.

Not far from the Statue of Liberty is Ellis Island. This was where the immigrants would disembark and stand for the first time on American soil. Between the years 1892 and 1954, Ellis Island was the headquarters of the Immigration and Naturalization Service of the United States. What happened on the island determined the future of each and every immigrant who landed there.

The main building on Ellis Island was a huge castlelike affair that echoed with the confusion of hundreds of voices, speaking different languages. It was filled with the noises of babies crying, officials barking orders, the shuffle of countless booted feet. The building was

almost as crowded as the ship the immigrants had just left—and as frightening. They lined up, waiting to be examined by the appointed doctors.

Ellis Island, seen from the torch of the Statue of Liberty. (Library of Congress)

"How is your hearing? Let me look in your ears."

"Open your mouth."

"Next! Next!"

"Take off your waistcoat and shirt. Do you have rashes? Lice?"

"Next! Next!"

Eyelids were turned inside out to check for trachoma while children screamed. Chalk marks told the story. This immigrant had typhoid. This one smallpox. This one was close to death.

Those who were sick but curable were taken to dormitories or to the island hospital. Those with contagious or "loathsome" diseases were sent back. Sometimes it was a child.

"But there is no one left over there to look after her. Oh, Stephen, we must go back, too!"

There were barrages of questions to be answered.

"Are you an imbecile?" Who among them would answer yes to that?

"Have you relatives here who will look after you if you need help? We don't want you if you will be a burden to the citizens of this country."

"We won't be. Let us in! Let us in!"

And millions were allowed in. By 1947, thirty million new immigrants had entered the United States through Ellis Island. The first was a young girl, Annie Moore from Ireland. She was given an American gold piece to mark the occasion. It was New Year's Day, 1892.

Annie Moore! The name was simple and went down in the his-

Immigrant women arriving at Ellis Island. (Library of Congress)

tory books. But some other names were "difficult" and were changed on the spot by indifferent officials when they filled out their forms. Schoenberner might become Shone; Riesman, Reese; Ivanovich, Evans, so that a name and a part of an identity was lost forever.

In 1924, the National Origins Act set limits on the number of people allowed to immigrate in any one year. It also established a "quota system" that stated how many people from each country would be allowed to enter the United States. It was not until 1965, more than forty years later, that President Lyndon Johnson signed into law the Immigration Act whereby all immigrants were admitted on a "first come, first served" basis. Those with family ties to American citizens were given preference.

Now it is a new millennium. And still they come, legally and illegally, every day of every week of every year. Pushed by the desire for better lives, they come across the borders of California and Texas illegally and dangerously. Newspapers tell pitiful stories of lives lost in failed attempts. If the illegals are caught, they will be sent back, one mile over the border, an often futile effort to stem the flow. Chances are, they will simply try again.

Most illegal immigrants from Mexico try to enter the United States by land. Others try to come by sea—Haitians, Nicaraguans, Cubans—risking their lives in small boats on an unforgiving ocean, their hopes set on Florida and freedom. They join new immigrants from Vietnam, Cambodia, and Russia, all of them seeking asylum in a safe haven.

Often the dream lives up to its promise. America is populated by businesspeople, shopkeepers, teachers, physicians, and homemakers with roots that go back, far and deep, to another land. They have enriched our lives.

For some, success exceeded their wildest dreams. Several of our presidents, including George Washington, were the sons or grandsons of parents who came from abroad. The great scientist, Albert Einstein came from Germany to settle in the United States. The remarkable dancer and choreographer George Balanchine came from Russia, as did composer Igor Stravinsky. Levi Strauss, whose first name decorates the jeans so many of us wear, was an immigrant from Germany. The list could go on and on. Anthony J. O'Reilly became president of the H. J. Heinz Company, all fifty-seven varieties. My husband and I remember Tony when he played rugby football for Ireland in the days of his youth.

Immigrants all. And aren't we all immigrants, too? Except for

Prospective U.S. citizens wait outside of the Immigration and Naturalization service with their paperwork. (UPI/Corbis Bettman)

Native Americans, didn't each person in this country originate somewhere in past time in another place, not here?

A nation of immigrants, indeed.

For those who come today there is not the heartache of total separation from family and homeland. There are jet planes and bargain fares and frequent-flier miles. There are fax machines, direct phone lines, video cameras . . . and credit cards that will let you go or buy now and pay later. Technology has broken down the barriers of space and time.

Since the beginning, immigrants have created pockets of home in their new land. There have been countless Chinatowns and Little Italys, as newcomers banded together for comfort and familiarity. Now there are more. Today, Korean immigrants can watch the twenty-four-hour Korean channel on their television sets. Russian immigrants can listen to a performance from the Moscow Concert Hall. The links with home are not entirely severed.

A mayor of Miami once said of that city: "You can be born here in a Cuban hospital, be baptized by a Cuban priest, buy all your food from a Cuban grocer, take your insurance from a Cuban bank."

The separation is easier perhaps. People, money, and ideas move from here to there and from there to here. We have become bi-continental.

When my husband, my three small children, and I dragged our-selves off that plane in San Francisco, weary and scared, we were met by a customs official. As he stamped our papers he said, "Welcome to America." They were the first words we heard spoken in our new country. I've never forgotten them or the kindness of that official's smile. Whoever you are, wherever you are, Customs Man, I thank you.

Many years later when I wrote my picture book *How Many Days to America?* I remembered him. When my fictional family, coming from a Caribbean country in a small boat, finally reaches land, the people on the dock call, "Welcome to America."

"But how did they know we would come today?" the father asks.

"Perhaps people come every day," the mother says. "Perhaps they understand how it is for us."

Perhaps they do. Or perhaps the family in my story was like us, blessed.

We prospered. My husband found a job. It wasn't easy, but he had faith and persistence, and like so many who came before him, he had a wife and children to support. And the signs that said NO IRISH NEED APPLY were only hateful memories of the past.

A tired immigrant rests.
(National Archives)

After waiting the necessary five years, he took the U. S. Citizen Petition Oath and became a "true American":

I hereby declare, on oath, that I absolutely and entirely renounce and abjure all allegiance and fidelity to any foreign prince, potentate, state, or sovereignty, to whom or which I have heretofore been a subject or citizen.

I was not personally acquainted with any princes or potentates, but it still took me several more years to "renounce." It's painful to give up your citizenship. In the end I did, and I'm proud to be an American. But still, when I hear "Danny Boy" sung or when I walk under cloudy skies, so like the skies of Ireland, my heart aches. When we plan a trip to visit our old country, we speak of "going home." When we are there, our vacation over, we speak again of "going home" . . . home to California.

Two homes, one here, one there. I think that is how it must be, forever, for the immigrant.

Eve Bunting was born in Ireland and lived there for the first thirty years of her life. In 1958, she moved to California with her husband and three children. She began writing in 1969, and her first book, a retelling of an Irish folktale, was published in 1972. Since then, she has written close to two hundred books for children and young adults. Ms. Bunting has received numerous awards and honors for her writing, including *Smoky Night,* which won the Caldecott Medal. Among her more recent books are *So Far from the Sea, Train to Somewhere, S.O.S. Titanic,* and *Going Home.*

AMERICA'S FIRST WORLD WAR

"It is not an army that we must train and shape for war. It is a nation. The whole nation must be a team."

—PRESIDENT WOODROW WILSON

Besides producing food to sustain life and raising a family to continue life, no human activity has consumed so much thought and energy as war, which destroys life. War takes different forms. There are wars between nations, civil wars, guerrilla wars, holy wars, revolutions, and terrorism. Yet, whatever the form, it seems as if there is always a war somewhere in the world. Historians estimate that only 268 years of the 3,421 years before 1968 were free of war.

No time has been more warlike than our own. The wars of the twentieth century have claimed (so far) a minimum of one hundred million lives. Their victims were often not military people killed in battle, but civilians. Millions died if they happened to be in the wrong place at the wrong time, such as a bombed city or a torpedoed ship. War also endangers a country's infrastructure—that is, the facilities a modern society needs to function properly. Among these facilities are factories and farms, transport and communication networks, water and power lines, and sewage systems. Starvation and disease always follow their destruction.

Americans fought in every major conflict of the twentieth century: World War I, World War II, Korea, Vietnam, the Persian Gulf War, and Kosovo. Their participation helped decide each war's outcome, thus influencing the course of world history. Yet that is only part of the story. Each war also changed the United States itself. To see how that happened, we must examine the first of these terrible conflicts. This is important, because the United States emerged from World War I as the world's leading economic power and, eventually, also its strongest military power. It holds those positions today.

World War I lasted from August 1914 to November 1918. It gets its name from the fact that, for the first time in history, fighting took place on a worldwide scale. Never before had a war involved nations from every corner of the globe. Simply put, it was a struggle for power in Europe and for colonies in Asia and Africa. On one side stood the Central Powers: Germany, Austria-Hungary, Turkey. Their opponents, known as the Allies, were France, Belgium, Russia, Italy, Japan, and the British Empire—Great Britain, Canada, Australia, New Zealand, South Africa, India. The war they waged was the greatest tragedy of modern times. We are still living with its consequences.

Never before had science and technology brought such misery to humanity. Airplanes, tanks, high explosives, long-range artillery, machine guns, submarines, flamethrowers, and poison gas took a frightful toll. About sixty-five million men served in the opposing armed forces, although not all at once. More than half—thirty-four million men—became casualties. These included twelve million killed or missing; "missing" nearly always meant that a soldier was blown apart, leaving no remains large enough to identify. Another twenty-two million were wounded, of which seven million became permanently disabled. In addition, roughly five million civilians died of war-related causes.

When war exploded across Europe, few Americans questioned the wisdom of George Washington's "Farewell Address." Upon leaving office in 1797, he warned against "entangling alliances," forming permanent military alliances with other countries because they might lead the United States into wars that were none of its business. Washington's warning became national policy, and the United States never fought alongside a foreign country. In August 1914, Woodrow Wilson, our twenty-eighth president, officially declared neutrality and asked Americans to be neutral "in thought as well as in action."

Despite the president's caution, it grew harder to stay neutral. The United States had always claimed the right to trade with any country it pleased, even in wartime. It called that right the "freedom of the seas." In 1812, it went to war with Great Britain to defend this basic principle. Germany, however, had its own ideas.

Since British warships prevented foreign goods from reaching the Central Powers, Germany retaliated by unleashing its submarines. Each month, these "U-boats," or undersea raiders, sank thousands of tons of British shipping. Finally, Germany announced that it would sink *any* ship, Allied or neutral, found sailing in British waters. That was a mistake. American public opinion was outraged at German "crimes," such as the 1915 sinking of the *Lusitania,* a British ocean liner carrying scores of American passengers. On April 6, 1917, President Wilson asked for, and Congress approved, a declaration of war. Although nobody knew it then, the United States had abandoned George Washington's policy forever.

Congress' action committed the United States not only to sending armies to fight thousands of miles from home, but also to mobilizing its home front to sustain them in battle. Europeans invented the term "home front" to describe a new reality: total war. When nations fought in the past, most civilians went on with their normal lives, unless they had the bad luck to live in a war zone. World War I changed all that. Huge armies and modern industry created total war. Now each nation had to harness every person and resource to the war effort. While military men used the tools of destruction, civilian soldiers used the tools of peace to produce whatever they needed. Home-front battlefields were factories, farms, mines, roads, and docks. Victory and defeat there decided the war's outcome as surely as the clashes of armies. The home front was subject to attack.

JOSEPH PENNELL DEL.

THAT LIBERTY SHALL NOT PERISH FROM THE EARTH BUY LIBERTY BONDS
FOURTH   LIBERTY   LOAN

Poster showing what will happen if Americans do not contribute to the war effort. (Library of Congress)

This was particularly true of France and Britain, where German warplanes bombed roads, railroads, and power stations.

It required a massive effort for America just to get into the fight. The country went to war with a volunteer army of eighty thousand men, tiny by European standards. Armed mostly with rifles and field guns, the army had few machine guns and no heavy artillery, tanks, or first-class warplanes.

To raise the necessary force, Congress passed the Selective Service Act requiring men between the ages of twenty and thirty to register for the draft. That was a bold move. During the Civil War, anger over the draft triggered riots in New York City in which hundreds lost their lives. Many Americans still regarded the draft as "military slavery" that turned wholesome youngsters into "heartless killing machines." Despite the opposition, draft boards took 2.8 million men into the armed services; another 2 million volunteered. Nearly half the total fought in Europe as part of the American Expeditionary Force (AEF).

America's home front had to supply them with everything they needed to live and fight. That meant solving enormously complicated problems, and quickly. Let's take a "simple" item like a bullet. The production of a bullet depended on using products and skills drawn from every section of the country. Montana copper miners, Connecticut brass workers, New York chemical makers, Delaware explosive technicians, Detroit machinists, New Jersey railroad crews: these and many others had to coordinate their efforts to make a bullet.

Bullets, however, were only one need. The nation had countless wartime needs, each with its own special difficulties. Yet meeting one set of needs meant shortchanging others that might be just as vital. Take, for example, nitrates, chemicals used in making both explosives and fertilizers. Should the limited nitrate supplies go into ammunition, without which guns are useless, or to grow food, without which gunners are useless? How much for each? Should new locomotives go to the AEF to haul shells to the front, or should they go to Chile to haul nitrates without which there would be no shells? These were complex questions, and they had no easy answers.

America entered the war as a jigsaw puzzle of industries, markets, transportation systems, and raw material sources. The business community lived by competition, each firm trying to buy and sell at the best price. Owners made their own decisions, in their own way, for their own benefit.

So did the government. Each agency had its own purchasing bureau, which vied with the others in buying whatever it needed. Thus, the office of the adjutant general, the War Department's chief legal officer, bought up all the typewriters it could find to keep the army and navy from doing the same. Similarly, the army's medical department cornered the market on canvas for stretchers, leaving nothing for combat soldiers' knapsacks.

Clearly, this was no way to fight a war. Victory required flexibility. It depended upon the ability to change as conditions changed. Instead of everyone competing with everyone else, Americans had to train themselves to see the "big picture." They had to think of their country as "Factory America," a unit operating under one efficient management.

Factory America's manager in chief was Bernard M. Baruch. Born in 1870, "Bernie," as friends called him, stood six feet four inches tall and had the body of an athlete; he kept in shape by boxing and lifting weights. A gentle, loving person, even as an adult he kissed his father in public. Yet he could also be as tough as piano wire. After getting his start as an errand boy for a New York stockbroker, he made his first million on Wall Street before the age of thirty. Since Baruch knew just about everyone in the business world, President Wilson asked him to head the War Industries Board (WIB).

Baruch became America's economic dictator. Only the president could overrule him, but never did. Within days of taking over, Baruch asked top business executives to help him run the WIB; few could resist a call from "old Bernie" to serve their country for the grand sum of one dollar a year. They began by making an inventory of the nation's resources. Then they decided how to distribute the resources in the best way.

Acting through his dollar-a-year men, Baruch sought to eliminate waste in the civilian economy and direct the savings to the war effort. He began by halting the manufacture of goods unnecessary for civilian well-being. Each saving, small in itself, added up. Baruch learned,

The War Industries Board. Its chief, Bernard Baruch, is seated at the lower right. (Library of Congress)

for example, that women's corsets had steel stays to make the wearers look slim. An order stopped corset making, saving enough steel to build two destroyers for the navy; corset factories switched to making stretchers for the army medical corps. Similarly, Baruch stopped production of brass and copper coffins. The metal saved went into bullets and artillery shells.

Baruch had many other products streamlined and simplified. Where others saw only a few inches of fabric or a tiny piece of metal, he saw vital military supplies. For instance, the backs of women's shoes reached over the ankles. By reducing the height, Baruch saved leather for the belts that held machine-gun bullets. Shorter women's skirt lengths translated into more cloth for uniforms; so did shorter men's coats, narrower lapels, and the elimination of outside pockets. Increasing the amount of thread on a spool saved wood for ammunition boxes. Wood replaced iron in baby carriages. Women's hairpins vanished from store shelves. Makers of bicycles, furniture, toys, and pocketknives had to redesign their products to save vital raw materials.

Each change created a "ripple effect." By freeing resources, it allowed the transfer of workers, machinery, and railroad cars to the war effort. Congress helped by passing a daylight-saving-time law.

This ordered the nation's clocks moved ahead in spring for an extra hour of daylight, saving coal and electricity. Businesses that cooperated made hefty profits guaranteed by the government. Businesses that refused to cooperate, or tried to cut corners, faced stiff fines and a cutoff of raw materials.

High war production required good labor relations. To get these, the president turned to the American Federation of Labor (AFL), which represented dozens of trade unions. In exchange for a no-strike pledge by the AFL leadership, he supported demands organized labor had been making for years, but without success. The president favored a minimum wage, an eight-hour workday, overtime pay, and insurance for work-related injuries—benefits we take for granted today. Best of all, he backed the workers' right to organize unions and bargain with employers. As a result, wages rose sharply during the war, and union membership soared from 2.7 million to over 4 million.

American farmers had a double task: feed their fellow citizens and the Allies. By early 1918, the Allies faced a desperate food crisis. Since millions of young men were fighting at the front, or the enemy occupied large areas of their countries, Allied food production lagged far behind their needs. In certain areas, at certain times, civilians suffered serious malnutrition, even starvation. Civilians in large parts of Belgium and Northern France, the scenes of great battles, suffered terribly in this way.

A month after the declaration of war, the president named Herbert Hoover head of the United States Food Administration. A mining engineer by profession, Hoover, like Baruch, knew how to tackle big problems. Unlike Baruch, he seemed cold and distant; nobody called him "Herbie," at least to his face. In 1929, he would become the thirty-first president of the United States.

Hoover's first task was to educate his fellow Americans about the importance of food as a weapon. Using the slogan "Food Will Win the War," he explained that they must save food, not by eating less, but by wasting less. People got the message. They began to "Hooverize" with wheatless Mondays and Wednesdays, meatless Tuesdays, and porkless Thursdays and Saturdays. Mothers learned not to overload plates at mealtimes and to remind children to "wipe your plate clean." Restaurants did not put bread on the table until after the first course, and then with just half a pat of butter per diner. Patriotic organizations collected garbage to recover anything useful to the war effort. Among these were fats for soap and glycerine for explosives; when burned, fruit pits and nut shells yielded carbon for use in gas masks. In one month, garbage from eleven cities produced enough glycerine for five hundred thousand artillery shells.

Hoover also wanted to raise more food for export. He urged farmers to bring every acre of their land under cultivation; no need to worry about flooding the market and lowering prices, because the government guaranteed top dollar for every bushel of grain and pound of meat. In 1918, Food Administration officials asked high schools in the Midwest to release boys over sixteen to help plant the spring wheat crop; each volunteer received full credit for the term. Similarly, city dwellers learned to turn backyards and vacant lots into "victory gardens," tiny vegetable farms. City schools "adopted" a school of the same size in an Allied country. Whatever food they grew freed an equal amount for shipment overseas. Even part of the White House lawn became a victory garden supervised by the president's new wife, Edith Bolling Galt Wilson.

Hooverization succeeded. Food savings and increased production soared to dizzying heights. Grain for making bread rose from under 3.5 million tons to 10.7 million tons within eighteen months, a record unequaled in world history. Meat and fats, essential parts of the American and European diet, leaped from 640,000 tons to nearly 3.5 million tons. Yet these are only cold statistics. Translated into war materials, however, they helped close the gap between victory and defeat. While German food production fell drastically, thanks to the cutoff of Chilean nitrates by a naval blockade, the Allies received massive shipments of American food. Without that food, the peoples of the Allied countries could not have kept up their war production.

World War I affected the lives of the nation's poorest. This was especially true of African Americans. In 1917, nine out of ten black people lived in the South. There, most black men worked as farmhands and unskilled laborers for sixty cents a day; black women worked beside them, or as housekeepers, for less. Worse, racial bigotry made their lives miserable. Segregation and mob violence robbed them of their dignity, kept them from voting, and prevented their children from getting a decent education. Then the war came.

The draft created a labor shortage. Hoping to expand their work-force, northern factory owners sent agents to recruit African Americans. Black-owned newspapers added further encouragement. The Chicago *Defender,* for example, constantly urged them to leave the South. "I beg you, my brother, to leave the benighted land," said a reporter in a famous editorial. "Get out of the South. . . . Come north then, all you folks, both good and bad. The *Defender* says come." Passed from hand to hand, and read aloud to those who could not read, the *Defender* reached vast numbers of people in the rural South.

Not since the Civil War, when slaves fled to invading Union armies, did so many African Americans pick up and leave. They left not only to earn more money, but to find dignity and freedom in the "Land of Hope," as they called the North. Perhaps seven hundred and fifty thousand black people boarded trains bound for Chicago, Detroit, Cleveland, and other industrial cities. Besides factory work, they took jobs in steel mills, shipyards, machine shops, railroad depots, and mines.

They did not find a warm welcome. Nearly a century before, in the years before the Civil War, Northern workers, fearing competition for jobs, rioted when free blacks settled in their communities. That sad history repeated itself during World War I.

"Jim Crowism," the systematic suppression of black people, reared its ugly face throughout the North. Race riots tore through two dozen cities and towns. Rampaging mobs killed black workers, burned their houses, and beat up their children. The worst riot took place on July 2, 1917, in East St. Louis, Illinois. "Riot," however, is not strong enough to describe what happened that day; perhaps "massacre" is a better word. Mobs surged through black neighborhoods, taunting the residents and screaming for their blood. When the smoke cleared, thirty-nine black people lay dead, including four children. Police officers watched from a safe distance, laughing as panicky blacks fled for their lives.

Despite hatred and violence, the newcomers found opportunities they had never had in the South. Northern schools were better than anything they had known before, and black people could rise above poverty in Northern cities. Wages were higher; in Detroit, the Ford Motor Company paid a fantastic five dollars a day. The war opened a door for African Americans that would never close. From then on, the civil rights movement grew as blacks refused to accept anything less than total equality. This was especially true of black war veterans. Some four hundred thousand black men served in the army. They were assigned to black, segregated units under white officers. As their grandfathers had done in the Civil War, the black soldiers served well and honorably. So, when they returned, they knew what they wanted.

Fenton Johnson captured their spirit in a poem. He called it "The New Day."

> *For we have been with thee in No Man's Land,*
> *Through lake of fire and down to Hell itself;*
> *And now we ask of thee our liberty,*
> *Our freedom in the land of Stars and Stripes.*

American women also gained from the wartime emergency. In many ways, all women, whatever their race, were second-class citizens. Although they formed more than half the population, they could not vote in national elections. In addition, dozens of occupations remained closed to them, not by law, but by custom, prejudice, and ignorance. Critics claimed that women were emotionally unstable, naturally "high-strung," and prone to "unreasoning hysteria." Men were supposed to be the exact opposites. Thus, building and repairing delicate machinery was man's work. Only men drove buses, sat at the throttle of locomotives, unloaded ships, delivered the mail, operated elevators, typed letters, and tapped out telegraph messages. Most telephone operators were men, as were nearly all doctors, judges, and lawyers. Even when a woman held the same job as a man, she seldom got the same pay.

Just as World War I opened opportunities for African Americans, it furthered women's struggle for equality. The labor shortage put women into jobs that few dared to imagine a few years earlier. About one million women joined the work-force for the first time. Not only did they take over traditional male jobs, they became "munitionettes"—workers in ammunition factories. That was no work for the meek and unstable. Munitionettes filled artillery shells with liquefied explosives and made detonation fuses, delicate tasks requiring both skill and courage, because a false move could blow a factory sky-high. Women who worked on the land were "farmerettes." Those who did not hold full-time jobs aided the war effort in countless ways. For example, ladies' clubs knitted scarves for soldiers, rolled bandages, and collected cooking fats, a source of chemicals for explosives.

More than twenty thousand women crossed the "Big Pond"—the Atlantic Ocean—with the armed forces. The majority belonged to civilian service organizations like the YMCA (Young Men's Christian Association), the American Red Cross, and the Salvation Army. Still others worked directly with the AEF as ambulance drivers, decoders, translators, clerks, and "Hello Girls," army slang for telephone operators.

Like their grandmothers during the Civil War, nurses served at the front and behind the lines in the sprawling military hospitals. These women knew the reality of war better than any stay-at-home man. It came as a terrific shock. They had volunteered expecting war to be neat and clean. Instead, they found horror, filth, and pain. Many had the same experiences as Vera Brittain, an English nurse. She wrote this after a battle in France:

A British poster encouraging women to sign up for work in a munitions factory. Without women workers, it would have been impossible to produce the shells needed by the artillery at the front. (The Trustees of the Imperial War Museum, London)

Gazing half-hypnotized at the disheveled beds, the stretchers on the floor, the scattered boots and piles of muddy khaki, the brown blankets turned back from smashed limbs bound in splints by filthy blood-stained bandages . . . beneath each stinking wad of sodden wool and gauze an obscene horror waited for me, and all the equipment I had for attacking it was one pair of forceps standing in a . . . glass half-full of methylated spirit . . . the enemy within shelling distance, refugee sisters crowding in with nerves all awry . . . gassed men on stretchers, clawing the air—dying men reeking with mud and foul green-stained bandages . . . dead men with fixed empty eyes and shiny yellow faces.

World War I changed not only the way women worked, but the way they appeared. Before the war, a "stylish" woman wore a tight corset under a high-necked dress with puffy sleeves and a hem that swept the ground. She piled her long hair, often reaching to the waist, into a huge bun crowned by a wide-brimmed hat kept in place with long pins.

This outfit went out with the war. It had to. Bernard Baruch's efforts to save cloth meant that women's clothes had to be streamlined. Equally important, the old-style dress was dangerous on a crowded factory floor. A wrong move might catch a sleeve or a hem, dragging its wearer into a whirring machine. As a result, dresses became shorter and more formfitting. Many women gave them up entirely in favor of pants. Easier to move around in and safer around machinery, pants have been popular with women ever since. So has shorter hair, which is cooler and requires less maintenance.

War work also gave women greater self-confidence. A steady job meant having one's own money to spend. That *was* freedom. For the first time in their lives, many women could make their own decisions without having to explain or apologize to anyone. Margaret D. Robins, an organizer of women's trade unions, captured the new spirit in a speech. "This is a women's age," she said. "At last women are coming into the labor and festival of life on equal terms with men."

Equality, of course, included the vote. Unless women got that, they could never be first-class citizens. Here, their wartime contributions carried more weight than all the arguments of all the feminists since the middle of the nineteenth century. By the time the war ended, few could deny that they had earned equality with men. President Wilson recognized this in a letter to feminist leader Carrie Chapman Catt. "The services of women during the supreme crises," he wrote, "have been of the most signal usefulness and distinction. It is high time that part of our debt should be acknowledged and paid." Congress agreed. In 1920, it passed the Nineteenth Amendment to the U.S. Constitution, granting women the right to vote.

Winning the war on the home front involved more than managing the economy and producing weapons. War is a contest—a deadly one, but a contest nevertheless. In war, as in sports, mental attitude is as important as material things. President Wilson understood that. He knew he could not simply order citizens to work and sacrifice for the war effort. To get the most out of them, he had to reach their hearts and minds. In short, Americans had to believe in their cause and want to give their all for it.

Reaching hearts and minds was the job of the propagandist. Unlike the teacher, whose aim is to help students grow by finding truth, the propagandist aims at shaping people's thoughts so that they act as he wishes. He may do this by telling lies, hoping these will not be discovered or discovered when it no longer matters. However, he may just as easily tell the truth, coloring it and slanting it to have the desired effect. All nations, including democracies, use propaganda in wartime. If done well, it strengthens their cause while weakening the enemy's.

President Wilson set up America's first official propaganda agency. Although he called it the Committee on Public Information (CPI), its aim was not to inform the people, but to sell them on the war. Wilson named George Creel, a gifted newspaperman from Colorado, as CPI director. He could not have made a better choice.

Creel leaped at the chance to try his ideas on a nationwide audience. As he saw it, the key to success lay in arousing emotions to a fever pitch. To do that, he said, he must fuse Americans into "one

As head of the Committee on Public Information, George W. Creel's job was to "sell" the war to the American public. (National Archives)

white-hot mass" burning with "devotion, courage, and deathless determination" to make any sacrifice the government asked. He called his own job "the world's greatest adventure in salesmanship."

A tireless worker, Creel was always on the lookout for creative ways to sell his product. At his direction, the CPI hired hundreds of writers, musicians, and actors to mount a propaganda campaign. The campaign went on every day the war lasted, reaching into every community except the most isolated. One thing was certain: If a community had a road, a CPI worker was sure to use it.

The Four-Minute Men led the way. These seventy-five thousand volunteers gave four-minute war pep talks in movie houses, theaters, ballparks, concert halls, schools, restaurants, hotels, railway stations, street corners—*anywhere* Americans gathered. They spoke on such topics as "Why We Are Fighting" and "The Meaning of America."

Creel went further. He ordered the CPI to stage exciting rallies, pageants, and parades. CPI printing presses churned out seventy-five million pamphlets to explain the "great crusade" from every angle and to praise America's role in it. CPI officials advised Hollywood on the type of movies it should make. Quick to see the connection between patriotism and profit, studios put out dozens of propaganda movies with titles such as *The Prussian Cur, The Claws of the Hun,* and *The Kaiser: The Beast of Berlin.* (Prussia was a large German state at the time, Huns were ancient barbarians, and the Kaiser was the German emperor.) Films like these changed the way children played. Boys gave up "cowboys and Indians" in favor of "Hunt the Hun" and "Hang the Kaiser." Girls gave up playing house in favor of playing a Red Cross nurse, caring for "wounded" dolls and kid brothers.

CPI songwriters cranked out every possible kind of war song. There were soldier songs like "Johnny Get Your Gun," "Good-bye Broadway, Hello France," "Over There," "My Buddy," and "I Don't Know Where I'm Going, But I'm on My Way." Songs urged women to urge their men to go to war. Mothers sang "I'm Proud to Be the Mother of a Soldier," "America Needs You Like a Mother (*Would you turn your mother down?*)," and "America, Here's My Boy." Young women chimed in with "What an Army of Men We'd Have If We

Ever Drafted Girls," "If He Can Fight Like He Makes Love (God help Germany!)" and "If I Were a Boy, You Bet I'd Belong to the Navy."

Creel even dragged God into the war effort. Clergymen of all faiths preached that God was "on our side." World War I, they said, was a holy war, a crusade in which every Allied soldier who died went to heaven the moment his soul left his body. America's cause was God's cause, according to one priestly poet. He urged fellow patriots to:

Fight for the colors of Christ the King,
Fight as He fought for you.
Fight for the right with all your might,
Fight for the red, white, and blue.

War propaganda aims at stirring up hatred for the enemy. A good way to do this, Creel believed, was through atrocity stories. An atrocity is a monstrous act such as killing or torturing enemy prisoners, the wounded, and civilians. Although such acts are illegal under international law, atrocities are as old as warfare. Whenever armies fight, there are bound to be violations of the laws of war. Governments may order them as a part of national policy of terrorism. Usually, however, individual soldiers and commanders commit atrocities on their own, without orders.

During World War I, American soldiers did some terrible things. For example, angry "Yanks" sometimes shot German machine gunners who fought to the last moment before raising their hands in surrender. Rather than expose himself to sniper fire, a Yank might "lose" a prisoner he was supposed to walk to the rear. Yet his government never ordered such acts, much less approved of them. If caught, he faced trial and punishment as a war criminal.

Germans committed far more serious war crimes. Local commanders terrorized civilians; they called it *Schrecklichkeit*—frightfulness. The idea was to crush any opposition to their advance. If, for example, civilian snipers fired at passing troops from houses in a village, the Germans burned the entire village, innocent and guilty suffering alike.

In the early days of the war, Belgium suffered horribly. Belgian civilians so resented the invaders that they began guerrilla warfare. Operating in small bands, they harassed the enemy by taking potshots at the troops and making surprise raids. The Germans struck back—hard. At Dinant, troops shot scores of hostages when their neighbors failed to turn in snipers. German troops also destroyed the city of Louvain, famous for its university and library, in reprisal for sniper attacks. Thousands of precious books, many dating from the Middle Ages, turned to ashes in a day.

Poster showing the "savage" German coming to America if people do not buy war bonds. (Library of Congress)

An old proverb says: "Truth is the first casualty of war." It is. The German record was bad enough, but not nearly as bad as Allied propagandists claimed. They used every trick to arouse fear and hatred of the enemy. Reports of Germans crucifying prisoners filled Allied newspapers. Unnamed "eyewitnesses" charged German soldiers with throwing Belgian babies into the air and catching them on bayonets; German pilots supposedly dropped poisoned candy and exploding fountain pens into French schoolyards. Propagandists even accused the Germans of collecting bodies from the battlefield, then grinding them up for fertilizer. As "proof," they offered forged letters and fake photographs. German propagandists did similar things.

George Creel believed a picture is worth a thousand words. In keeping with that belief, he enlisted the nation's artists for propaganda work. Through the CPI's Division of Pictorial Publicity, painters, illustrators, and cartoonists shocked the nation with gruesome, blood-curdling images. Their works showed the Germans not as people, like themselves, but as beasts in human form. In doing so, they hoped to frighten Americans into making any sacrifice to win the war.

Cartoonists drew pictures of children crying because Germans had cut off their hands "for sport." Poster artists created bold, yet simple, images to catch the eyes of busy passersby. Posters came in all sizes, from that of a sheet of newspaper to a billboard the size of a barn door. Some posters made simple requests: SAVE FOOD, BOOKS FOR THE ARMY, DON'T HOARD COAL. Others urged citizens to buy Liberty Bonds to pay for the war.

Bond posters were shockers, leaving little to the imagination. One showed German bombers flying over New York Harbor. Below, the Statue of Liberty stands headless, engulfed in flames, her torch lying at her feet. The caption reads: THAT LIBERTY SHALL NOT PERISH FROM THE EARTH—BUY LIBERTY BONDS. In a poster titled REMEMBER BELGIUM, a German soldier grabs a girl of eleven or twelve by the hand; she wears only a nightgown, and he is dragging her into the shadows. In DESTROY THIS MAD BRUTE, a hideous ape wearing a German helmet carries off a screaming woman. Other posters had titles like HALT THE HUN and BONDS OR BONDAGE.

Only days before delivering his war message, President Wilson told a newspaper editor about something that had been bothering him ever since the trouble with Germany began. "Once lead this people into war," he said, "and they'll [the American people] forget there ever was such a thing as tolerance. To fight you must be brutal and ruthless, and the spirit of ruthless brutality will enter into the fiber of our national life, infecting Congress, the courts, the policeman on the beat, the man in the street. Conformity would be the only virtue, and every man who refused to conform would have to pay the penalty." Most of all, he feared that the Constitution, the foundation stone of American liberty, would crack under the stress of total war. If that happened, the nation would become just like the enemy.

Before running for political office, Wilson had been a professor of history. Wilson's study of the past taught him valuable lessons. It convinced him that a nation at war is like an iron chain consisting of millions of separate links. Now, just as a chain is only as strong as its weakest link, a nation's strength depends upon the unity of its people. To question a war's justice or necessity, to urge others to refuse to help the war effort, weakens the home front. And since the home front supports the armed forces, snapping those human links opens the way to defeat. For that reason, it becomes difficult to protect civil liberties when they may undermine the war effort.

President Wilson's fears were justified. He had once said the United States had gone to war to defend democracy. Yet the war quickly turned into the harshest test of democracy ever experienced by the American people. Not even Wilson himself was immune from the hysteria against which he had warned. He did nothing to calm the wartime frenzy that gripped the land.

World War I showed Americans at their best and at their worst. Millions believed in the Allied cause and supported it with dignity and a respect for civil rights. However, millions of others, normally sensible people, saw Germany as the root of all evil. They hated fellow Americans—*good* Americans—simply because they spoke German, or because their ancestors came from Germany generations ago. Much of this hatred was expressed in silly, ignorant ways. German measles got a new name—"liberty measles." Sauerkraut became "liberty cabbage," and hamburgers, "liberty sandwiches." Dachshunds turned into "liberty hounds," and German toast, "French toast."

Saloon keepers removed "Hunnish" pretzels from their free lunch counters. Libraries took German books and record shops took music by German composers, off their shelves. Colleges stopped teaching German, calling it the language "of brutality and hatred." The town of Berlin, Iowa, changed its name to Lincoln, and Cincinnati's German Street became English Street. German family names like Ochs and Schwartz became Oaks and Black.

Anti-German feeling also had a more dangerous side. The First Amendment to the Constitution guarantees freedom of speech. The right to speak one's mind is sacred; no democracy can survive without it. Before World War I, federal authorities never had the legal power to interfere with what citizens said in public. Congress changed all this by passing the Espionage Act of 1917 and the Sedition Act of

1918. These laws made it a crime to use "disloyal, profane, or abusive language" about the American government, military, or flag. In other words, anyone who disapproved of the war, or said anything an official did not like, automatically became "un-American." Violators faced fines of up to ten thousand dollars and as much as twenty years in jail.

The government prosecuted more than twenty-one hundred people under these acts. It denied use of the mail system to magazines and newspapers critical of the war; it shut down some and jailed their editors. Teachers who refused to take loyalty oaths lost their jobs. One man went to prison for laughing at draftees, another for speaking too loudly during a patriotic ceremony. New York police tapped telephone lines without obtaining a court order, as required by law. A California judge sent film producer Robert Goldstein to prison for ten years. His crime: making a film about the American Revolution. *The Spirit of '76* showed Patrick Henry defying Great Britain and the Boston Massacre in all its gory detail. Nobody denied that these events had taken place; schoolchildren read about them in their history books. Yet dramatizing them in a movie was a crime during World War I because it might show our British ally in a bad light.

Private citizens took matters into their own hands. Self-appointed true-blue patriots joined groups with names like the Knights of Liberty, the Liberty League, and the American Rights League. The American Protective League (APL), the largest group, boasted of two hundred and fifty thousand members. Headquartered in Chicago, the APL had branches in every major city from coast to coast. Its members became an unofficial secret police force dedicated to uncovering spies. There *were* German spies in the United States, but they were not a serious threat. Within days of the declaration of war, federal agents arrested most spies; those who remained at large went into hiding, fearing for their lives. No matter. Wherever Americans gathered, APL members tried to overhear their conversations. APL school visitors encouraged children to report anything "suspicious" they heard. On the testimony of his five-year-old daughter, a California man received five years in prison for criticizing the president in the privacy of his own home.

You did not have to say anything to draw attention to yourself. Always on the alert for "suspicious" behavior, APL members impersonated federal agents, carried out illegal searches, and made "citizens" arrests. Eagle-eyed patriots paid special attention to "gloaters," those who seemed to enjoy hearing about enemy successes. In short, sneaks, busybodies, tattletales, and snoopers had a grand time during the war to save democracy. Nevertheless, they found not one spy. President Wilson never challenged them or said a word against them—at least not for the record.

One did not have to be a traitor to oppose the war. Thousands of decent people believed their country had no business meddling in a foreign war—and surely no right to have its youth massacred on foreign battlefields. Both sides, they insisted, cared more about gaining colonies and making profits for big business than human rights. Ordinary Americans had no stake in this war, they said, but were its victims. Europe's war was Europe's affair. If Europeans wanted to fight, let them do it with their own sons. Eugene V. Debs, leader of the American Socialist Party, described the conflict as "a rich man's war and a poor man's fight." He insisted that every dollar spent on the war meant a dollar less for America's poor. Several labor unions, notably the Industrial Workers of the World (IWW), called for strikes to gain higher wages and better working conditions.

The government saw these critics as threats to national unity and thus to the war effort. In reply, it sent Debs, convicted of violations of the Espionage Act, to prison for ten years; he received a pardon after the war. Justice Department agents staged massive raids on IWW offices across the country, jailing hundreds of its leaders. The IWW never recovered from these attacks.

Private citizens went even further. Newspapers reported scores of incidents where "patriots" broke the windows of stores owned by shopkeepers with German-sounding names. In other incidents, mobs whipped or tarred and feathered critics of the war.

At least two men died. In Butte, Montana, a mob kidnapped Frank Little, an IWW organizer. It tied him to the back of a car, dragged him through the streets until he bled all over, then hung him from a railroad trestle. A coroner's jury ruled that "unknown persons" had committed the murder, and that ended the investigation.

In Collinsville, Illinois, rumor had it that German-born Robert Prager was storing dynamite to blow up a coal mine. He was not; in fact, he had tried to enlist in the navy, only to be turned down for medical reasons. A mob seized Prager, wrapped him in an American flag, and hung him. The police arrested eleven men for the crime. During their twenty-five-minute trial, the accused wore red, white, and blue ribbons in their buttonholes. A defense lawyer said they had done nothing wrong; it was all right to commit what he called "patriot murder." The jury agreed. After acquitting them, a juror shouted, "Well, I guess nobody can say we aren't loyal now."

Victory came on November 11, 1918. Compared to the millions of Europeans who died, American losses—totaling 75,658 in eighteen months—were trivial. Nevertheless, World War I had important effects on the United States.

Woodrow Wilson had called it the "war to end all wars," fought "to make the world safe for democracy." It did neither. In examining the long-term results of *any* war, we find a "mixed bag." No war has ever brought forth a perfect world. Nor has it condemned humanity to everlasting agony. Nothing lasts forever. Good and evil come and go. That is the way of the world.

World War I set the stage for the rise of murderous tyrannies in Germany, Russia, Japan, and Italy. Within a generation, those tyrannies plunged humanity into World War II, followed by the Cold War with Communist Russia. These conflicts were direct outgrowths of the twentieth century's first great war.

That war also revealed dark currents that would break the surface of American life throughout the twentieth century. Thus, the East St. Louis massacre foreshadowed the murder of civil rights workers in the 1960s. Similarly, the death of Frank Little anticipated the assassination of Martin Luther King, Jr. In each case, men died because others saw those with different ideas as threats to the social order.

The official and unofficial persecution of Americans of German origin, "spies," and "traitors" anticipated the anti-Communist hysteria of the 1950s. Those were the years when Senator Joseph McCarthy and the House Un-American Activities Committee bullied and persecuted fellow citizens in the name of anticommunism. Like the earlier American Protective League, this new crop of "patriots" imagined "traitors" lurking under every bush, ready to overthrow American democracy by armed force.

World War I left yet another legacy, but a more positive one. It furthered the cause of civil rights for black people, feminism, and better conditions for working people. By doing so, it pointed to a brighter future for all Americans.

Albert Marrin has written thirty-one nonfiction books for young people and is currently chairman of the History Department at Yeshiva University in New York City. Prior to teaching at the college level, he worked for nine years as a social studies teacher in a public junior high school. There, he welcomed the challenge of finding ways to make history come alive for his students, and he continues to meet this challenge as a writer. Among Dr. Marrin's most recent books are *Unconditional Surrender: Ulysses S. Grant and the Civil War,* which was a *Boston Globe*-Horn Book Honor Book, as well as *Commander and Chief: Abraham Lincoln and the Civil War* and *Terror of the Spanish Main: Sir Henry Morgan and His Buccaneers.* A native New Yorker, Albert Marrin lives with his wife, Yvette, in the Riverdale section of the city.

A Hundred Years of Wheels and Wings

In the spring of 1901, Connecticut farmer Abel Hendron hitched his team of horses to the wagon and began the 7.5-mile journey to town to pick up a plow ordered in February. Ordinarily, it could take him anywhere from two to four hours to reach town and come home, not counting stops he might make along the way to chat with neighbors.

Hendron considered himself a modern farmer and kept a record of farm-related matters in an effort to be as efficient as possible. His journal entries were usually spare and to the point, but on this day, the entry seems especially so: "Left at 7 and all went well to Sudley's [farm] where road turned soft from [previous two days'] rain. Looked to be very deep mud near stream and so turned back. Washed horses and wagon. Two hours gone."

While Hendron's experience was frustrating, his means of transportation was typical for the beginning of the twentieth century. Most travel and hauling within cities and towns, and between the more isolated towns and villages, was still accomplished by horsepower. Coal, ice, milk, furniture, medicine, and a variety of other goods were delivered in horse-drawn wagons. Doctors visited patients by horse and buggy. Fire equipment was pulled by teams of horses. Coffins were conveyed to cemeteries via horsepower, trailed by a line of mourners in horse and carriage. Horses also provided the power to pull plows and threshers, as well as to haul crops to the nearest market or storage facility. In short, the nation depended on its over fifteen million horses for its day-to-day survival.

Of course, the horse was not the only way to move goods and people in the early 1900s. The two-wheel, safety bicycle had come into its own after 1885 and provided a measure of individual travel freedom. But bicycles were leg driven, left the rider exposed to all weather, were not at all safe on ice or snow, and could not easily carry oversized items—all of which limited usefulness. And since most roads were made either of cobblestone or dirt, the ride was anything but smooth. Even so, there were over one million bicycles on those bumpy roads in 1900.

Steamboats, an early nineteenth-century invention, still plied waterways, but they had severe limitations. They could travel and dock only where the water was deep enough; they cost a great deal of money to operate, especially when going against a strong current, and they had no other choice but to follow a river's route, thus leaving most people too far away from them to be of daily use.

And there were the railroads. By 1900, the United States had built over one hundred and ninety-three thousand miles of mainline railroad track, by far the most of any country in the world. Ribbons of steel linked thousands of cities and towns with forty thousand locomotives pulling over forty-five thousand passenger cars and an astounding two million freight cars from one side of the country to the other.

Railroads were the fastest-growing transportation industry in America then, and yet they, too, had troublesome drawbacks. Track, engines, and cars were incredibly expensive to build, operate, and service. Trains ran on fixed schedules along fixed routes, which made them inconvenient for short-haul work, such as delivering items within a town. Finally, despite widespread track coverage, the great majority of America's seventy-six million people did not live within walking distance of a station—and, thus, were still dependent on their horses.

An offshoot of the train, the electric trolley, aided intercity travel, but had the same general drawbacks as its big brother when it came to routes and schedules. Besides, many people did not enjoy traveling on a trolley while crowded shoulder to shoulder with strangers.

But another way to travel existed at the dawn of the century. It was a relatively new invention and went by many names back then: the quadricycle, the automotor, and the horseless carriage to list a few. In time, the machine would come to be called an automobile or, for those who liked a less formal name, the car.

The automobile had been all the rage in Europe since 1886 when a German engineer, Gottlieb Daimler, put a lightweight engine in a four-wheel carriage. The 1.5-horsepower engine poked out the rear floor awkwardly, but the thing could speed along at an incredible ten miles per hour! America's fascination with the horseless carriage would not begin until Frank Duryea and his brother Charles built their own gasoline-powered automobile in 1893.

Between then and the new century, American engineers tinkered and refined their machines. They tested out cars powered by steam engines, electric motors, and the internal combustion engine (where an explosion of gasoline inside a metal cylinder produces the energy to turn the wheels). Despite improvements, American cars were still little more than metal and wood buggies with engines stuck in them. A few builders actually included a whip with every sale in case the owner needed a horsepowered tow back to the barn!

If style was not an important design factor, neither was comfort. Cars were usually steered by tiller, though even with a steering wheel turning was a clumsy chore. Tires were often made of hard, solid rubber that sent a bone-jarring jolt to passengers every time they hit a bump. Engines were loud, car-shaking affairs that discharged noxious fumes and often stopped running for no apparent reason.

These machines, automotive historian Ralph Stein notes, were "a horror on wheels. The brave eccentric who owned one happily put up with its crankiness if the beastly thing would only run. It was unbelievably difficult to operate and control, and when it wouldn't run nobody knew how to fix it."

Early driving enthusiasts had to accept the finicky nature of their machines and, more often than not, had to deal with the complex and messy mechanical workings themselves. The manual for the 1903 Cadillac contains this rather daunting receipt for care of the chain that turned the rear wheels:

About once a month, the chain should be taken off the sprocket, soaked in gasoline, and cleaned with a stiff brush to remove grit and dirt. Then take four pounds of beef tallow, a pound of graphite, and one pint of heavy lubricating oil. Heat and stir. When thoroughly melted, dip the chain into the hot mixture, leaving it there long enough so that it soaks into all the small bearings. Then let the chain drip, wipe the outside, and replace on the sprocket.

To ignore these instructions was to risk snapping the chain and having a long walk home.

Of course, any auto trip out of town during this period could turn into an unwanted adventure. There were no gas stations, car mechanics, or motels back then, and very few roads had route markers to guide a motorist from one town to another. Travel of any distance in a car was so chancy that one automotive magazine urged drivers to carry a basic

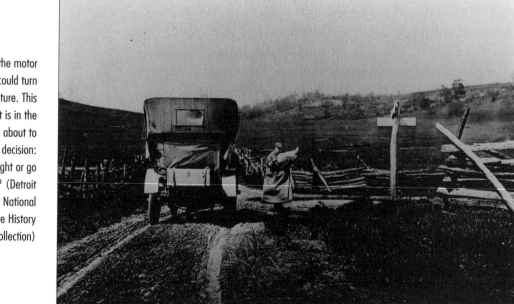

At the dawn of the motor age, every trip could turn into an adventure. This plucky motorist is in the middle of nowhere about to make an important decision: Should he turn right or go straight ahead? (Detroit Public Library, National Automotive History Collection)

outfit of thirty-five tools, forty-eight spare parts, and an emergency food supply that included four gallons of water, four pounds of hardtack (compressed, hard crackers), four tins of meat or fish, and two pounds of chocolate.

As if the cars themselves weren't a big enough problem, a small, but vocal, number of people complained that the automobile was an undesirable intruder. Several doctors worried that the physical strain of driving one of the newfangled machines would cause "acute mental suffering, nervous excitement, and circulatory disturbances." Many rural citizens complained that a car's loud chugging and frequent explosive backfires scared horses or caused cows to stop giving milk.

Groups formed to combat the mechanical invader. One particularly pesky organization was the Farmers' Anti-Motoring Society in Pennsylvania. In the early 1900s, it issued a set of rules it hoped the state government would adopt. One proposed rule stated: "If the driver of an automobile sees a team of horses approaching, he is to stop, pulling over to his side of the road, and cover his machine with a blanket or dust cover which is painted or coloured to blend into the scenery, and thus render the machine less noticeable." The same group also wanted night drivers to fire off Roman candles every mile and then wait at least ten minutes so the road ahead could be cleared of other traffic.

Local and state politicians found themselves under great pressure to regulate automobiles, and they responded with a profusion of traffic laws. Most early laws were reasonable and designed to maintain safety for drivers and pedestrians, as well as for the many animals that inhabited the nation's cities and villages. Some, however, were meant to discourage automobile driving altogether. A 1902 Vermont ordinance required that an adult walk at least a quarter mile ahead of every auto waving a red warning flag, while Tennessee motorists were expected to put up a written notice one week in advance of any trip.

In general, drivers chose to ignore the more outlandish laws and suggestions, in part because they knew they could easily escape the police, who were often mounted on bicycles.

The biggest factor threatening to keep the automobile a mechanical curiosity was its cost. The price of a car ranged anywhere from $1,000 to $3,000, with some going for over $5,000. At a time when the average worker in the United States earned around $650 a year, and a very comfortable house $2,500, there weren't many people wealthy enough to own an unreliable, uncomfortable toy. One magazine, *Country Life in America,* found that it was cheaper to own a team of horses and two well-made carriages for a year than to drive a "first-class American Automobile for four thousand miles." As a result, there were only eight thousand cars in the United States in 1900.

But even as Abel Hendron was plodding toward town and frustration on that spring day in 1901, a change in the automobile was taking place. The Olds Motor Works, founded and run by Ransom E. Olds, introduced a new car to the auto-buying public, the Curved-Dash Oldsmobile.

The 1901 Oldsmobile was a tiny, lightweight machine that carried two people and boasted a 5.0-horsepower engine neatly tucked away under the seat. Pneumatic (air-filled) tires and large springs front and rear softened a ride that could, on a straight, level section of road, reach a breathtaking 20 miles per hour (breathtaking, in part, because there was no windshield to deflect rushing air, bits of debris, or bugs).

The car was also very reliable, at least when compared to the other forms of personal transportation available. Advertising for this model showed a hapless man struggling unsuccessfully to harness a stubborn, rearing horse, while nearby a perfectly composed couple toodles along the road in their handsome Curved-Dash. The ad's text exclaims boldly:

NATURE MADE A MISTAKE IN GIVING THE HORSE BRAINS. SCIENCE DID BETTER AND MADE THE OLDSMOBILE MECHANICALLY PERFECT—PRE-SUPPOSING BRAINS IN ITS OWNER.

Finally, and most important, Olds had the engine and many of the car's parts built in one area of his factory, and then he brought them to another where they were assembled. This early form of mass production saved so much expensive labor time that he was able to offer his car for just $650.

In its first year, a respectable 425 Curved-Dash Oldsmobiles were sold. The next year, sales jumped to 2,100. By 1903, this model accounted for one-third of all car sales in the United States, with 3,750 rolling out of the factory. The machine was so popular and beloved that Vincent Bryan and Gus Edwards wrote a hit song about it called "In My Merry Oldsmobile."

Why did the automobile survive and flourish despite its many drawbacks? When it worked, a car did away with having to own, stable, care for, and control a bothersome horse, yet it allowed for the same sort of unrestricted personal travel. What is more, women—even the most refined and dainty—discovered a sense of freedom they'd never had before. A car powered by an electric motor could be switched on easily, could run very quietly, and could cover from fifty to one hundred miles between battery charges—as long as the speed was held down to about twelve miles per hour.

For men, freedom of travel was nice, but more alluring were the speeds a car could reach. An advertisement for the 1907 Ford Runabout promised, "You can jog along mile after mile and enjoy the scenery. Of course you can scorch if you want to—forty miles an hour easily." Meanwhile, F. E. and F. O. Stanley made international headlines when their specially designed steam-powered Stanley Rocket broke five world records in 1906 and finally reached a speed of 127.6 miles per hour. One year later, the Rocket racing car topped itself with a speed of 197 miles per hour!

As sales increased, more and more companies began to manufacture automobiles. One directory for a 1912 national auto show listed fifty-four separate manufacturers of gasoline cars (and this did not count the makers of electric- or steam-powered autos). Car names familiar to us today, such as Ford, Buick, and Oldsmobile, could be found side by side with such obscure ones as Wolverine, Elmore, Pungs-Finch, and Zent.

As the building of cars went from incidental tinkering to a robust industry, so did the competition for attention and sales. Advertising played a part in this, but it was the very real improvements in the cars themselves that sold them. Automobile makers built stronger, more reliable engines. They designed air-filled tires that didn't fall off the rims after hitting a bump. Hardtops, with doors and windows, shielded riders from wind and the elements. Automatic electric starters did away with the sometimes dangerous hand-cranked starter. Brakes were improved, and lights were made brighter.

Henry Ford's Model T could carry people, milk cans, produce — anything that could fit in it. It could even be jacked up and used for a varitey of farm chores, such as grinding grain. (Collections of the Henry Ford Museum and Greenfield Village)

Without doubt, the automobile advanced more in the opening years of the twentieth century than at any time before or since. "By 1914," Ralph Stein writes, "the automobile was, in almost every respect, as good as the car standing in your driveway right now."

While the automobile was being dramatically improved mechanically, two other changes took place that would guarantee automobiles a place in the lives of nearly every American. One was the introduction of the boxy little Model T by Henry Ford in 1908. Ford had been building cars since 1896, always striving to create what he referred to as "a car for the great multitude." With the Model T, that car was born.

While the first Model T was criticized as ugly and somewhat difficult to operate, it proved to be an extraordinarily practical machine. Farmers found that its high axles let it bounce over the worst ruts and plow through mud and water even while lugging a sizable load of milk cans or vegetables. If they attached steel wheels to the rear, it could even be used as a tractor. Firefighters lengthened the chassis to make it into a hook and ladder truck. The post office found it the most reliable way to carry mail along rural routes. Fords were also fairly simple machines to repair, and the company made sure that spare parts were readily available everywhere in the United States.

The first T was somewhat pricey at $850. But Henry Ford was a fanatical follower of the principles of "scientific management" as put forward by Frederick W. Taylor. Ford began by giving each worker a specific task to perform in the assembly of a car. One worker fit tires to the wheel rim, another attached the wheel to the axle, while yet another bolted the axle to the chassis, and so forth. No longer did a worker have to know how to assemble every part of a car. Later, Ford applied the idea of continuous motion, using conveyor belts, gravity slides, and overhead monorails to feed parts to the machinery where workers stood. When Ford began, it took almost twelve and one half hours to build the car's chassis. By early 1914, he'd gotten the time down to one hour and thirty-three minutes.

By 1924, Ford's mass-production assembly plants were producing nearly nine thousand cars every day. (Collections of the Henry Ford Museum and Greenfield Village)

As production speeded up, the price of the Model T went down. By 1912, it cost $600; by 1918, it was $450. When the 1924 Model T appeared, it cost just $290! Nearly nine thousand T's were rattling off the assembly lines every day by then. In all, 15,456,868 Model T's were produced between 1908 and 1927, when it was finally replaced by the Model A.

Lower prices put ownership of a car within reach of just about everyone, and in short order, other companies went to assembly-line manufacturing. Unfortunately, the expense of building the colossal mass production plants drove most of the small car makers out of business or forced them to merge with the larger corporations of Ford, General Motors, and Chrysler. Many highly distinctive luxury car models would be produced over the years, but the low-priced "car for the great multitude" would be the driving force of the industry.

As great as Ford's contribution to the automobile was, probably the greatest boost to its dominance came from one of the least glamorous aspects of driving. The road.

At the opening of the century, America's roads were, quite literally, a mess. The busiest streets in most cities might be paved with cobblestone or brick, but side streets were still bare dirt topped with oil or gravel. Outside of towns, the dirt road—some 2.5 million miles of it—was the rule. One Iowa resident recalled that "when it rained, you were stuck [in mud], your wagons, your feet, you just stayed in your house until it dried. That could be two, three weeks, a month."

Calls for better roads had been around long before the automobile. Farmers had always complained about the wretched condition of their roads, but very little was ever done to improve them. One bicycling group, the League of American Wheelmen, began lobbying state governments in the late 1880s for "improved roads," and the group even managed to get several states to organize road commissions. But real road building in America had to wait until the American people and Congress saw that a strong economy was directly linked to decent roads.

This happened after Congress commissioned a series of studies to

Early drivers had to be a hardy breed, often because of awful road conditions. This one ponders the dilemma of his mud-stuck auto and knows he'll probably require horsepower to get it rolling again. (Brown Brothers)

determine the importance of roads. One report found that, because of poor road conditions, an American farmer paid twenty-one cents in labor and time to haul a ton of produce, while a French farmer paid just eight cents because of smoother roadways. In addition, the nation's 3.5 million car owners and 250,000 truck owners now saw their vehicles as vital to their work—and they were important enough politically to get real action. In 1916, President Woodrow Wilson signed into law the first Federal Aid Road Act, which had the federal government paying for half the costs of road improvement and construction by individual states.

States went into a road-building frenzy, covering existing streets, roads, and frequently used back routes with concrete and asphalt. Eventually, the states would produce over four million miles of paved roadways. The federal government got into the road building business itself in 1954 when President Dwight D. Eisenhower signed the Federal Aid Highway Act, initiating the construction of the forty-thousand-mile Interstate Highway System.

As state and national road systems grew, thousands of gasoline stations, garages, restaurants, and motels sprouted along them to service and fuel the increased traffic. More and more people took to the roads as travel became faster and easier—and car buying took off. In 1920, there were approximately nine million cars in the United States. Ten years later, that number had leaped to nearly twenty-seven million. By 1995, over ninety percent of all American households had at least one car, with most families owning two or more vehicles.

Today, a complex network of asphalt and concrete links together every region of the country. Goods can be shipped five hundred miles overnight by truck, and families can travel by car or bus to other states with an ease that would have been shocking just forty years ago. In the two hours Abel Hendron wasted, he could now cover one hundred and twenty miles!

Of course, there was a real downside to having more cars and roads in the United States. Many people decried the arrogant way in which state and federal road builders seized land and divided—and sometimes destroyed—communities and cities with strips of ugly pavement. Others bemoaned the fact that cars and highways meant businesses and upper- and middle-class families could more easily flee urban centers for the suburbs, leaving behind aging buildings and some of the nation's poorest citizens. And there is little doubt that our swarms of cars and trucks have created traffic congestion, added to air pollution, and made us dependent on foreign sources of oil.

One of the saddest changes was the sharp decline of the railroad (and the virtual disappearance of the trolley). At the beginning of the century, railroads were an American institution and an economic force. But as more cars took to the road, ridership on trains and trolleys fell dramatically, and railroads began to shrink in size and importance. The following comparison over five decades shows how steep that fall has been:

	1930	1980
Miles of operating track	429,883	290,000
Locomotives in operation	56,582	28,396
Freight cars in operation	2,276,867	1,710,827
Passenger cars in operation	52,130	4,347

Since 1936, passenger operations have made a profit only during World War II, when the government curtailed auto travel.

Trains could still carry many bulk products, such as coal or iron ore, very economically, but they found themselves losing business to trucks when it came to smaller items or quantities. A 1918 Mack Trucks ad told clearly why this happened: "Full-powered, like a giant locomotive, the MACK truck . . . follows no prescribed track but moulds its routes according to the demands of transportation."

Adding to the railroad's decline was another form of transportation that appeared during the car's struggling infancy. On December 17, 1903, Orville and Wilbur Wright managed to pilot their flimsy, two-winged flying machine on a series of wobbly flights, the longest of which lasted 59 seconds and covered 852 feet. They were the first to demonstrate that flight of a heavier-than-air machine was possible, and yet their achievement was noted in only two newspapers across the entire nation.

Five years later, when the Wright brothers demonstrated an

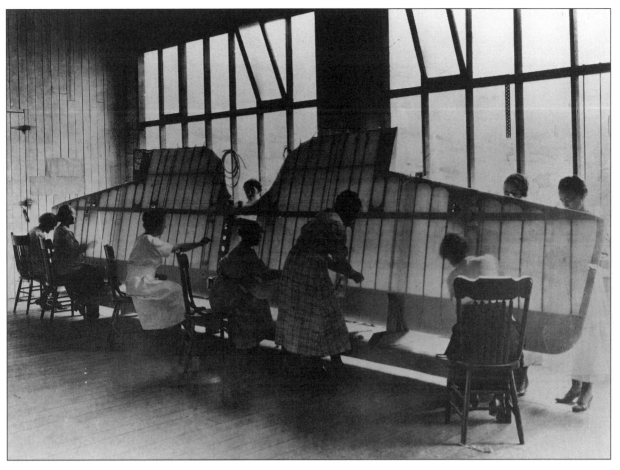

improved version of their airplane that stayed aloft for over two hours, the world finally took notice. Humans were indeed flying!

What followed paralleled the development of the automobile. Enthusiastic tinkerers borrowed and improved upon the Wright brothers' basic design principles and built their own flying machines. Glenn Curtiss had his two-winged "June Bug" up in the air in 1908, and Clifton O. Hadley got his homemade triplane airborne in 1910. For every machine that succeeded, there were scores of others that failed miserably. J. S. Zerbe attempted flight in his quintaplane, an imaginative assembly of five wings, metal tubes, and wires that never left the ground.

The period leading up to and including World War I was a time of rapid change for the airplane. More powerful engines were built, handling was improved, canvas was wrapped around the body to protect

Early airplane construction was done by hand with few tools. Here a team of nine women attach the thin fabric to the top wing of a bi-plane. (Boeing Aircraft Company)

During the 1920s, most Americans experienced the wonders of flight by watching barnstorming pilots do loop-the-loops, power dives, and other stunts. For added thrills a smiling Lillian Boyer enjoyed hanging from a wing at seventy miles per hour. (Minnesota Historical Society)

the pilot and help the plane move through the air more smoothly. During World War I, the federal government became involved in the assembly-line production of the famous Curtiss JN-4, also known as the "Jenny." The government would be intimately linked with the design and development of all flying machines from this time on.

While the airplane was improved a great deal, it remained a strange and frightening curiosity in the eyes of most people. The planes of the time had an extremely bad reputation for crashing—and for good reason. They had no radio and no navigational instruments, and pilots often veered off course or encountered sudden, violent weather changes. Flight was so dangerous that thirty-two of the first forty pilots to fly the mail from New York to Chicago were killed in crashes.

Plane builders insisted that most crashes involved old, worn-out machines being flown recklessly by daredevil pilots. Their new planes, they insisted, could stay aloft for hours on end and were extremely safe when flown carefully. However, the public remained skeptical of the plane as a source of transportation until May 1927. That was when a tall, slender airmail pilot (and survivor of four plane crashes himself) named Charles A. Lindbergh flew his single-engine plane from Long Island, New York, to Paris, France, thus becoming the first person to fly nonstop across the Atlantic

Ocean. When the wheels of his plane, *The Spirit of St. Louis,* touched down in Paris, Lindbergh became an instant celebrity of international proportions—and the age of air transportation truly began.

Reliable, safe air travel brought distant cities closer and made far-away, exotic lands suddenly accessible. The first coast-to-coast passenger service was launched in 1929, and combined plane travel during the day with train travel at night. It was a grueling two-day journey, but it still saved travelers a full thirty-six hours over the fastest express trains. When night flight was made safe, the train part of the trip was dropped, and the railroads lost even more riders as a result.

As passenger flight grew more profitable, fledgling airline companies went through the same sort of growing pains as the auto industry. The high cost of designing, testing, and mass-producing new planes and airport facilities led one builder after another to merge with a larger manufacturer. By the mid-1930s, Douglas DC-3s were carrying people across the United States, while Martin China Clippers hopped from island to island in the Pacific. These early passenger planes were cramped, uncomfortable, noisy boxes, but this didn't stop eager passengers from boarding them in increasing numbers.

Passengers board a United Airlines Ford Tri-Motor plane late in 1931 for a journey to an island in the Pacific Ocean. (National Air and Space Museum, Smithsonian Institution)

To encourage those still reluctant to fly, airlines and plane makers launched an all-out promotion campaign, touting the speed and safety of air flight. The Ford Motor Company—which for a time made airplanes as well as automobiles—claimed its "Stout-Ford all-metal plane is the safest in the world" and could attain a speed of ninety-five miles per hour. For those who still refused to fly, Ford prodded them along with this reminder: "Those who hesitate to employ the airplane will do well to recall that there are still many old-timers who refuse to ride in automobiles!"

Following World War II, improvements in commercial airliners

When the Boeing 247 was introduced, its all-metal, low-wing construction was so unusual looking that it drew crowds of curious onlookers. (Boeing Aircraft Company)

were generally linked to military-funded research. The wing design for the World War II B-17 bomber was later utilized by Boeing to make planes for Pan American Airline's transatlantic service. Radar, originally developed to detect enemy ships and aircraft, was used to guide planes to airports and help them avoid midair collisions; the first strategic jet bombers (the B-47 and the B-52) were redesigned to become the first U.S. commercial jet, the Boeing 707. And it was military rocket technology that eventually led to manned spaceflight and the first moon landing in July 1969.

If Abel Hendron took a ride to town today, he would probably drive a pickup truck or an off-road four-wheel-drive vehicle. It would have a quiet one-hundred-and-fifty to two-hundred horsepower engine, power steering, power windows, power brakes, a comfortable bucket seat, and climate control.

He would travel along nicely paved streets, roads and highways, listening to news or music and occasionally waving to neighbors. He would have no problem with mud or roads so rutted as to be impassable, though a traffic jam could certainly slow his pace.

In all, his travel time for the round-trip journey of fifteen miles might be a half hour to forty minutes, depending on how fast he drove and how many red lights he might catch along the way.

He would probably be startled to learn that the auto had replaced the horse in the lives and hearts of most Americans and that only a tiny handful of determined farmers still used them for work. He would certainly be shocked to see the sky filled with all sorts of metal birds carrying people to every corner of the world. He might even blink in disbelief if someone told him that tests were being done on cars that moved over roads without wheels and on passenger planes large enough to hold eight hundred people.

But Abel Hendron considered himself a modern farmer. So he would have driven quite happily into the twenty-first century, ready for whatever new forms of transportation the future might hold.

————

Jim Murphy writes: "I grew up in the small industrial town of Kearny, New Jersey, and spent most of my time playing baseball and football, exploring abandoned factories or wandering along the banks of the Passaic River. I 'discovered' books (and my love of history) when I was around twelve years old and have been an avid—if not fanatical—reader ever since. After college, I was a children's book editor for seven years and then became a freelance writer. Since then, I've published about twenty-five books, most of them nonfiction, which focus on the people and events that have shaped American history. Among them are: *Gone A-Whaling: The Lure of the Sea and the Hunt for the Great Whale; A Young Patriot: The American Revolution as Experienced by One Boy; The Great Fire;* and *Across America on an Emigrant Train.*

THE CENTURY BABIES BECAME PROS

During the twentieth century, American sport escalated from games played for free, out of sight of anyone but the players, to the status of a great cultural allegory for everything from military strategy to morality. Today, games are played for millions (of dollars and of fans)—by athletes of both sexes and any possible race, which wasn't possible at the "national hero" level until midcentury.

Players become huge media stars as a matter of course and often behave with a bizarre "I'm special, I live by different rules" attitude, even as parents wail that they should behave as moral "role models." Meanwhile, many kids who play the games of which these athletes are the elite want to strive for this flashy elevation as much as they want to—well, just *play* splendidly. Quite often, this striving is not originally the kids' idea, but that of their push-push parents.

This situation applies to dozens of sports in the year 2000. The game-playing elite used to be more exclusive: in the early part of the century, America really had only one king-making game— professional baseball, as played by only white men. (There were "Negro Leagues" that matched many African-American players of superior ability. But although the excellence of the play in these leagues has been recognized belatedly, during the era of segregation "majority America" limited the glory of "the national pastime" to the whites-only sport.) From major-league baseball, kids and adults drew heroes and loyalties outside the run of their school-day and work-day lives.

Baseball players performed baseball feats within the realm of seasons (154 two-hour games) and baseball championships. Jillions of followers—even troops abroad from World War II on—leaned close to their radios as critical games unfolded. Star players drove fancy automobiles, wore snazzy clothes, smoked fat cigars around which they grinned at the newspaper cameras. In short, the players of this game—which mean essentially nothing in the large scheme of world progress—showed off their money and general cultural grandeur with a kind of innocent pre-TV vanity that invited the fans to both envy the stardom and vicariously enjoy it.

But on the field, to those who paid the small ticket price to see them firsthand, the players and what they did seemed athletically marvelous but somehow still *human*. In the 1930s, the pitcher Carl Hubbell invented the screwball—a pitch that broke the other way from a curveball—and threw it so often that when he let his arms hang, his left (pitching) hand rested *palm outward* along his thigh. Now, *that* was a *human* arm, a willful deformity anyone could feel in his own bones and shake his head at. When Babe Ruth (sixty homers in 1927) rotated that cooper's-dream of an ungainly barrel torso and flicked another ball over the distant fence, then trotted with a surprising daintiness around the bases, his strength seemed all the more understandable to the fans for its being generated by such a plain old, oddly overweight body.

As the century rolled on, other games—basketball, football, tennis, golf, ice hockey, soccer—developed big-time professional levels of play. But even in these sports (and even after desegregation), as in baseball, the life stories of the athletes, for quite a few generations, exemplified the same kind of comprehensible *humanness* as the players ascended to their game's highest standards. Pros were usually just grown-up kids who fell in love with their game at the age of ten, twelve, fifteen, whatever, and played a lot, practiced more and more, showed a growing talent as the years went by, and finally rose through tougher and tougher competition to find themselves, almost suddenly, sliding into third base in Yankee Stadium, or charging the Centre

Court at Wimbledon, or fading a 7-iron shot onto the green of the sixteenth hole at Augusta National.

Again, these were *human* stories. Not to sound ridiculous, but the fans and the kids who played the games in their schoolyards, or on their frozen ponds, or on public courts could easily identify with the pro players as being of the same *species* as they themselves, could *feel* that the athleticism on display was, however great, still something attainable—or at least something that could be playfully copied. Because we're all just human beings, right? It's just that some of us have a little extra talent, or opportunity, or something comprehensible to lifelong amateurs.

Let me jump ahead here for a second to ask: Do you feel, readily, without a second's hesitation, that you are of the same species as Monica Seles? Michael Jordan? Wayne Gretzky? Tiger Woods? John Elway? Nolan Ryan? Diego Maradona?

I bet you hesitated there. Because these people are all otherworldly in their pure greatness; the purity of their talent is such that they almost seem like aliens bred from birth to be the star performers they have become (on the field, never mind on camera for the moment).

Wayne Gretzky: Just your normal, everyday 10-year-old who scores 378 goals in 67 games. (Hockey Hall of Fame)

Well, the truth is that, with the exception of Jordan, they *were* bred almost from birth to be the best players in the sport they would later dominate—and dominate by huge margins, leaving everyone else way behind. But it wasn't Martians who decided when she was four that Monica would be a tennis phenom; it wasn't on Jupiter that the two-year-old Gretzky was put into ice skates and two years later was playing hockey in a league of eight- to ten-year-olds; it wasn't a Saturnian golf club that Tiger's father wrapped his son's *ten-month-old* hands around. These decisions for future greatness were made at these incredibly early ages by the parents of the future stars, and they were bred to that greatness right here on good ol' Earth.

By the last years of the twentieth century, the early-breeding phenomenon had spread to the point that, by 1999, virtually *any* player on a major-league team or on the big-time golf and tennis circuits was someone whose parents had planned just this future for their kid and had started his or her training, usually with considerable rigor, before the kid was six or seven years old. These athletes' *whole lives* have been dedicated to reaching the highest level of play in their game.

As the ages at which the elite athletes started training got younger and younger, the level of skill needed to compete for a spot in the big time got higher and higher. In fact, the skills became almost incomprehensible, inhuman. The pro players moved farther and farther away from the vast number of fans and amateurs and once-hopeful kids watching or playing the game on rather understandable boy-and-girl levels—especially after television interposed itself between us and the stars and made it possible for them to earn outrageous sums of money.

Let's face it. Wayne Gretzky *is* an alien.

The growing distance between the highest-level pros and the kids who play pickup games or recreation-league seasons is not necessarily a bad thing, except for those boys and girls who find their childhood sacrificed on the altar of possible future stardom. I have a son who plays a few sports at the travel-league level, and at each of his games, there are a few hyperachieving kids being driven by bellowing perfectionist parents. And I can tell you: By the time they are twelve or so, most of these kids are pretty tired of dominating every game in which they play and wish they could kick back and chill out sometimes. High pressure at home can get to you; and, conversely, the on-field mental coolness these kids develop eventually deadens the game-to-game enthusiasm for most of them. How many hat tricks can you get before a hat trick becomes ho-hum?

As I watched Tiger Woods walking up the eighteenth fairway on the last day of the 1997 Masters tournament—with a *ten*-stroke lead, for goodness' sake, at the age of what?, twenty-two, while the announcers chirped about his father (who stood by the green, unsmiling to the point of severity, erect, arms crossed, no sentimental foolishness now) having twisted his baby's fists around a 6-iron at ten months—I thought, *Young fellow, you play beautiful golf, but, oh, how I pity you.* Me, I was playing with a rattle at ten months, as were my sons, neither of whom will ever win the Masters by ten strokes at twenty-two, but both of whom, like millions of other kids, went from a rattle to a stuffed bear to a plastic truck, and when they decided they wanted to learn how to play a sport or two because it looked fun, learned it and played it exactly as long as it stayed fun.

This isn't reverse snobbism or a phony "proletarians are the real guys" attitude. Nor am I suggesting that Tiger doesn't enjoy golf. But I bet he didn't figure out his putting-practice routine when he was two all by himself, in the natural course of things. And I bet he *has* figured out by now that when you win the Masters by ten strokes at twenty-two, you're looking forward to a very long future in which you will be expected to achieve an unreasonable perfection, in public, by jillions of people, and you're looking backward wondering where your childhood went while your dad was hollering at you about wrist pronation on the backswing. I'm just guessing. But to me, the sweet-looking kid walking as a winner up the fairway was literally bred to walk up as a winner, toward the stern father whose physical attitude seemed to say, *Yes, this is only what you were supposed to do.* Well, I like Tiger, but the whole thing struck me as being kind of sicko.

A friend of mine insists that Tiger Woods has become an inspiring icon for kids, especially African-American kids, to begin playing golf.

How many Tigers does the next century hold? (Alan Levenson/Corbis)

But I believe that for every kid who begins playing golf because of Tiger, there are five who say to themselves, *But he started when he was ten months old. I'm nine years old already! I'm way too old—why bother?*

The same friend claims that television, instead of making sports stars into media stars and games into mere TV shows that we watch one huge step removed from the humanness of the athletes, actually breaks down barriers between us and them by making their games so widely broadcast, so easily watchable. I think he's full of beans. When you watch MJ make a great reverse layup, and then immediately watch it four more times from different angles in slo-mo, the improvised, split-second shot becomes something that feels artificial. Every time it is shown again, it seems more and more choreographed for the camera. Like the rehearsed touchdown dance of the wideout or the knee skid of the goal-scoring striker, the action has become a piece of goods, not much different, emotionally, from a pair of sneakers.

I keep thinking back to the 1987 Masters—ten years before Tiger's—in which the affable new golf god Greg Norman, the grimly concentrated two-time Masters champ Steve Ballesteros, and local Augusta boy Larry Mize, a slight, weak-chinned fellow who would have made a fine Good Humor man with a white paper cap, finished in a tie and set out for a play-off. All three represented the old-style, easily believable human story: Norman learned golf knocking a ball around the hardpan of Australia; Ballesteros played for years in his decidedly golf-unfriendly Spain with only one club, a 5-iron, with which he drove, chipped, and putted; Mize, a caddy, used to sneak over the fence to catch a little of the Masters' practice rounds when he was a lad. (Larry seemed as if he had sneaked over *another* fence to get into this play-off with these two relative giants.)

On the first hole of the play-off, Norman hit a terrific approach shot and tapped in a par putt; Mize sank a gutty ten-footer for *his* par. Then, alas, the almost viciously proud Steve lipped his four-foot par putt and thus was eliminated. A long, sad walk back to the clubhouse for him. Mize and Norman moved on to the next hole, a par three with water in front of the green, which sloped severely toward the drink.

Mize hit first off the tee and struck what must have been golf history's sorriest clutch shot—a shanked iron that splayed so far right (and uphill) of the green that it was almost out of bounds. Norman—whose instinct was always to go for every pin, a recklessness that lost him several tournaments—watched Mize's ball finally stop in the hinterland. For once, however, recalling the caution advised by his self-appointed mentor, Jack Nicklaus, Greg went *against* his killer instinct and dropped his tee shot within the fat part of the green, forty-five feet away and slightly downhill from the cup. From there, he could easily finish in two putts, without having to stroke the ball toward the water. Mize, up and away off under the longleaf pines, could easily take six shots to finish, probably all of them stroked *toward* the water.

Larry, of course, hit first. Faced with impossible trouble, he pulled a duffer's no-no. His chip, which should have been bladed beneath the ball so it would rise high and bite into the sloping green with enough backspin possibly to stay out of the water, instead popped off his club like a Rod Carew single. It never rose above four or five feet, hit the ground running, and kept on going. It was no doubt the *second*-worst clutch shot in gold history, doomed, certainly, to plug deep into the Georgia mud of the creek bottom.

But Mize had done one single thing perfectly: He had hit the ball dead on the line for the pin. And as millions of disbelievers—including Larry himself—watched, the ball struck the pin, and slid right down the pole into the cup. Birdie for Larry, who, with incredible good grace, bounded only two or three times in joy before settling down and begging the crowd to keep quiet so that Norman could concentrate on holing the forty-five-footer he had fatally left for himself.

Norman looked like a man crawling out of an overturned car just after a nasty multivehicle smashup. He missed his putt by five feet. Then he went over and hugged Mize, who was almost apologetic about making his shot, a humility Norman would not accept. He kept telling Larry what a great shot it had been, great shot, great shot.

Well, Norman was being a staunch kind of guy, but the fact is, it was a *horrible* shot. It turned into a beautiful, flukey, deus ex machina victory; but the fabulous result—and the credit Mize deserves—doesn't change the fact that, when the heat was on, homeboy Larry did what most of *us* would do. He choked as if he'd swallowed a chicken bone: whaled his drive into the next county, then spanked the tar out of a ball he should have feathered.

And, as has happened on occasion to every amateur who has played golf or any other game, he got lucky. In his case, his boo-boo turned into what could be regarded as the greatest clutch shot in golf history. (*I* regard it as such and find it wonderful that even the pros—Mize was an excellent pro—need pure luck sometimes.)

That long, winning chip was a great shot—and Larry was the kind of guy we could feel was as human as we are. At the award presentation, the Augusta chairman had the unspeakable rudeness to say, as he handed Larry his green jacket, "Well, it wasn't as exciting as last year, but here you are." The year before, Nicklaus, who had been playing golf since he was about five, had won his (ho-hum) sixth Masters (by one shot, over the same snakebit Greg Norman). I, and I bet a lot of duffers everywhere, and kids learning the game, and fans in general, were outraged by the crude insult. What could be more exciting than seeing a normal sort of guy hit the same awful kind of shot we might hit and yet score the most unlikely of victories? (And I was rooting for Norman, to boot.)

Larry Mize after striking the greatest, ugliest, clutch hole-out shot in golf history. (UPI/Corbis-Bettman)

Former NBA guard Glenn "Doc" Rivers once told me, "You know, there are probably two or three *million* kids out on basketball courts across the country right this minute, convinced they are going to get to play as a pro." He shook his head. "Now, I am the last person to step on somebody's dream and determination—but do you know how many jobs open up in the NBA in a given year? Maybe fourteen? Maybe eighteen? That's two million cut down to eighteen. Those are not numbers to give up everything else in your life for."

That same year, I drew my son Alex's attention to a big article in the *Washington Post*'s sports section, with a headline something like

KIDS SHOULD CHOOSE ONE SPORT BY AGE EIGHT, PLAY IT YEAR-ROUND. At the time, Alex played soccer in the fall, ice hockey in the winter, lacrosse in the spring, and baseball in the summer. In between all of these, which he played with a number on his back, he fit in days during which he would play pickup basketball or street hockey or go skateboarding, often for six or seven hours straight.

Alex read about half of the article, then casually dropped the paper. "What do you say?" I asked.

"Oh," he said, with slight sarcasm, "it's for kids who want to get *really good*." He gave a brief laugh. "As opposed to kids who want to have a lot of fun."

The heart of American sport, as it has evolved in the twentieth century, and as will be made increasingly evident in the early twenty-first, is not necessarily exemplified by Mark McGwire and Dennis Rodman and Mia Hamm and Michael Chang and Tiger Woods and their like, amazing and admirable though some of the stars may be. The specialization and early-training regimen recommended by the *Post* has brought in a sort of athletic caste system, and these people are the far-away elite, the Brahmins, the gentry. Gripping their little golf clubs at ten months old, lacing up their ice skates at two, they leave most of us way behind as confirmed amateurs, out simply to have a bit of good ol' human fun. They leave us all to act like kids, especially when we happen to *be* kids. There's nothing wrong with this. Adults can exemplify dreams fulfilled; who else but kids ought to exemplify *play*?

Frankly, healthy though it is to strive to gain skill, I think most of us are probably better off enjoying our games on our own scale. But just once, I'd like to dunk with both hands.

––––––––––

Bruce Brooks grew up in North Carolina and Maryland. He has written two Newbery Honor Books: *The Moves Make the Man* and *What Hearts,* as well as twenty other books of fiction and nonfiction, including the twelve-novel *Wolfbay Wings* ice hockey series. He has two sons, Alex and Spencer.

PENNY COLMAN

GREAT STRIDES:
Women in the Twentieth Century

During the early 1900s, Helen May Butler was the first woman leader of an all-woman brass band. Wearing colorful, stylish uniforms, Butler and her Ladies Brass Band performed throughout America and in Argentina and Germany to great acclaim and financial success. They played at fairs, expositions, amusement parks, and concert halls—203 times in Boston, 110 times in Buffalo, 126 times in St. Louis, and 130 times in Charleston. Typically, there were twenty-five to thirty-five young women in Butler's band who played brass instruments, woodwinds, and the bass drum. Although many of the musicians left each season to get married, they were quickly replaced from a long waiting list of eager women musicians.

Butler conducted the band, played the solo cornet and violin, and composed music. In 1904, President Theodore Roosevelt used her march, "Cosmopolitan America," as the official theme music for his reelection campaign. After Roosevelt's inauguration, Butler and her band played her march in a command performance at the White House. By then, the sheet music for "Cosmopolitan America" billed it as "The Nation's Hit!" and "The Most Widely Played March in Existence."

Helen May Butler was openly proud of her all-female band. In her advertisements, she did not hesitate to inform people that her band was the "first all women's brass band and female leader . . . [the] only

Holding her baton, Helen May Butler posed with the members of her very popular Ladies Brass Band. (Smithsonian Institution)

band in America independent of men's tuition and assistance . . . equal in ability to any of the men's bands."

Butler was one of a growing number of American women who were feeling confident and carving out careers in the first decades of the twentieth century. It was a time when extraordinary changes were transforming the nation. Telephones, automobiles, and indoor plumbing were replacing letter writing, horse-drawn buggies, and outhouses. Industrialization was replacing agriculture. Urban areas were growing bigger than rural areas. Millions of immigrants continued to arrive. In its mail-order catalog, Sears, Roebuck & Company told its customers, "We Have Translators to Read and Write All Languages" and included samples of German, Spanish, Dutch, Italian, Polish, and Czech.

Other women who were seizing new opportunities included Maggie Lena Walker, who, in 1903, started St. Luke Penny Savings Bank in Richmond, Virginia, and became the first woman bank president. In 1911, Blanche Stuart Scott, known as the "Tomboy of the Air," started her career as a pilot. That same year, Jovita Idar de Jaurez organized the Mexican Feminist League in Texas and used her skills as a journalist to advocate for equality. In 1918, Dorothy Johnson got her first job at the telephone company in Whitefish, Montana. "Not everybody had a telephone—at $1.75 a month on a four-party line, it was a luxury that lots of people could do without . . . I started at age fourteen . . . because I needed that money to help pay for an education."

The new freedom many women felt was, in large part, the result of years of struggle by previous generations of women to change attitudes, customs, and laws that had traditionally confined and controlled them. By the turn of the century, there had been a dramatic increase in educational opportunities for women. Most married women could own property, keep their own wages, sign legal documents, and sue for a divorce and custody of their children. Women factory workers were demanding better wages and working conditions.

Women now engaged in activities such as roller skating, bicycle riding, golfing, playing tennis, and canoeing. Women's fashion was moving away from tight corsets and hoop skirts. The new look was represented by the "Gibson girl," a creation by illustrator Charles Dana Gibson that appeared in magazines. The Gibson girl wore her long hair up and preferred shirtwaist dresses, flared skirts, blouses with trim collars, and simple straw sailor hats. Typically, she was portrayed bicycling, sailing, or holding a golf club or a tennis racquet.

Despite the changes, women were still denied suffrage, or the right to vote, in most states. Since the first formal demand for the vote was made at the First Women's Rights Convention in 1848, waves of women had worked to win the vote. Now a new generation of more militant women devised new tactics—open-air meetings, huge suffrage parades, cross-country trips in automobiles, and a dirigible balloon with a large silken banner inscribed VOTES FOR WOMEN. On January 10, 1917, women started picketing the White House. Standing in silence, they held banners that read, MR. PRESIDENT, HOW LONG MUST WOMEN WAIT FOR LIBERTY?

Three months later, the United States entered World War I. Many women joined the war effort. Hundreds of women drove ambulances in Europe. Thousands served as nurses. Millions of women went to work making war materials and doing every other available job. Although they were criticized for being unpatriotic, women continued picketing at the White House. The messages on their signs pointed out that while America was fighting for democracy abroad, American women were denied the right to vote at home. "This was often embarrassing for the president, and the police were given orders to stop the picketing," recalled one woman.

The police arrested many of the women and charged them with obstructing sidewalk traffic. At least 168 women were sent to jail. Edna Mary Purtell, a nineteen-year-old file clerk, was arrested four times in one day and spent five days on a hunger strike in jail. Women who went on longer hunger strikes were brutally force-fed. This was done by holding a woman down and shoving a tube down her throat. According to one account, "Pictures began to appear (in newspapers) of women being carried out of prison on stretchers or being just able to walk. . . . These women, of varying position, wealth, age, and education . . . endured filthy jails, vile food, and hunger strikes to get what they felt was their inalienable right."

After World War I ended in 1918, women intensified their efforts to win the vote. Finally, in 1919, Congress passed the Nineteenth Amendment to the U.S. Constitution that stated: "The right of citizens of the United States to vote shall not be denied by the United States or by any State on account of sex." The amendment was ratified by the necessary number of states and became the law of the land on

A suffragist picketing in front of the White House in 1917. Suffragists often wore a white dress and a sash with purple and gold, the colors of the suffrage movement. (UPI/Corbis-Bettman)

August 26, 1920. Celebrations took place across America. On August 27, the morning newspaper in Pittsburgh, Pennsylvania, announced that the mayor had declared a "joyous" noontime celebration. As the clocks struck twelve, a resounding chorus of shouts, cheers, factory whistles, car horns, and church bells erupted throughout the city.

During the 1920s, many characteristics of modern America took hold. Electricity was widely used for lighting, cooking, and household appliances. Consumer goods galore were being produced—cars, pianos, refrigerators, toasters—and widely advertised as never before. The cosmetic industry began to boom. Over the course of the decade, an average American woman went from buying virtually no cosmetics to buying a full pound of face powder and eight separate rouge compacts.

A new way of buying—installment buying—was being touted. In earlier years of the century, consumers had to pay "cash on the line." Now they were told, "No need to wait. You don't need the ready cash—you can get and enjoy right now the merchandise you want—and pay for it while you use it."

New devices of mass media—radio and the movies—were creating a mass culture by transmitting images, messages, and experience to huge numbers of people anywhere in America. According to Kate Simon, who was eight years old in 1920, "The brightest, most informative school was the movies. We learned how tennis was played and golf, what a swimming pool was and what to wear if you ever got to drive a car—and of course we learned about Love, a very foreign country."

The 1920s have been called the "Roaring Twenties," and for some women they were—in particular, for young women known as "flappers" who wore bright red lipstick and their hair bobbed short, tweezed their eyebrows, shortened their skirts, drank, and smoked. Because part of the look was a slim, boyish-type figure, some flappers bound their breasts to make themselves look flat. Bernice Stuart Snow recalled the time that her young aunts from Portland, Oregon came to visit her family in Huron, South Dakota: "They came back with real short dresses above their knees, stockings rolled down beneath their knees, and high heels. They had the new hairdo. They smoked cigarettes. You weren't considered a nice girl if you looked like that. The town was scandalized."

Clara Bow came to epitomize the flapper when she starred in the 1927 silent film *It* (a euphemism for sex appeal, coined by the English writer Elinor Glyn). Bow became known as "the It girl." In most of her movies, she played the role of a young working woman who acted liberated by smoking, drinking, dancing, and wearing short skirts but who really was a "nice" girl. The movie would end with Bow's character's morals still intact, leaving her job to marry "Mr. Right."

Many women made their mark in the 1920s. Bessie Smith's first record, "Down-hearted Blues," sold more than two million copies. Gertrude Ederle swam the English Channel and set a speed record that beat the male record by almost two hours. Women led the picket lines at a strike of the textile mills of Gastonia, North Carolina. Ynes Mexia traveled from Alaska to the Amazon in search of rare plants. Dorothy Eustis opened the first Seeing Eye school, where she trained dogs and blind people to work together. The author Dorothy Canfield Fisher attended a dinner in her honor at the Author's Club of New York. According to Fisher, "This is the very first time they have offered a dinner for a woman writer and they are going to continue to do so from now on, so they say. How many doors are opening up everywhere for women!"

Doors slammed shut, however, when the stock market crashed in 1929 and catapulted America into the Great Depression. Banks went out of business. Factories and mills closed. Millions of people were unemployed. Farmers lost their farms. Homeless families scrambled to find shelter. Hungry people scrounged for food. Wong Wee Ying, who lived in Midland, Pennsylvania, made soup out of rice or oatmeal and vegetables from her garden and clothes out of rice sacks for her children.

Married women who managed to have jobs were criticized for taking employment away from men. The popular opinion of the time was that it was a man's responsibility to support his family financially. Women, in particular married women, were barred from jobs in many school districts, banks, insurance companies, and utility companies. They were, however, hired to do work that most men would not do such as sewing, cleaning, and certain sales and clerical jobs. Women also took in boarders, started household beauty parlors, returned to canning and baking, and made over old clothes.

In 1932, Franklin Delano Roosevelt, who pledged to bring a "New Deal" to the American people, was elected president. His wife, Eleanor Roosevelt, was very active with political and social issues. After his election, Roosevelt appointed Frances Perkins secretary of labor. Perkins was the first woman ever to serve in the cabinet. She worked closely with the president to develop federal programs that would help people.

One program, the Federal Arts Project, was designed to create jobs for writers, musicians, artists, actors, and photographers. Since discrimination in hiring was prohibited in this program, a record number of women were hired. Zora Neale Hurston collected folklore and edited oral histories. Eudora Welty took photographs in rural Mississippi. Alice Neel and Louise Nevelson created murals, prints, and sculptures. Augusta Savage and Gwendolyn Bennett ran the Harlem Art Center.

Four women were among a group of artists who were hired to paint fresco murals on the inside of Coit Tower, a prominent landmark that still stands on the top of Telegraph Hill in San Francisco. Among the murals that tourists today enjoy is Maxine Albro's scene of California agricultural life that shows workers in the orchards, the vineyards, and the flower industry, where one woman is depicted holding a freshly cut bundle of calla lilies.

In the midst of the hard times, Americans were led, inspired, and captivated by outstanding women. Babe Didrikson set three world records and won two gold medals and one silver in track and field at the Summer Olympics. Jane Addams and Pearl Buck won Nobel Prizes—Addams for peace and Buck for literature. Mary McLeod Bethune headed a federal agency that helped African- , Mexican- , and Native-American youth. Amelia Earhart made the first transatlantic solo flight by a woman. At the movies, where the price of admission was ten cents, fans flocked to see women stars such as Bette Davis, Katharine Hepburn, and Greta Garbo.

One movie star, Ginger Rogers, was featured as the "Ideal Girl" in the 1935 Sears, Roebuck & Company mail-order catalog. Shoppers who wanted "a flat tummy" could choose from a number of corsets that Rogers had "autographed." They could also order "Ginger Rogers lace panties" for forty-five cents. According to the catalog, "No wonder Ginger Rogers chose this clever little panty for herself! Three rows of the sweetest lace trim at bottom." The use of the word "panty" was a first in a Sears catalog. In early catalogs, such items were called "drawers."

The economic hard times ended in 1941 when the United States entered World War II. As millions of men went off to fight, stereotypes about what women could and could not do were suspended. Suddenly, women workers were wanted everywhere—in shipyards, aircraft factories, munitions plants, and government offices. Women joined police forces, drove taxicabs, and ran farms. Women lawyers, astronomers, architects, geologists, and journalists were in demand. A new word—"womanpower"—was heard on the radio and seen in newspapers and magazines.

Women did what needed to be done to help win the war. They worked in defense industry jobs and civilian jobs. They served as Red Cross volunteers, air-raid wardens, fire watchers, messengers, and drivers. Hundreds of thousands of women joined the military. They taught all-male classes in instrument flying and gunnery. Women nurses landed with the troops on the beachheads of North Africa. Women journalists and photographers covered every aspect of the war. Among the best known was Margaret Bourke-White who slept in foxholes, flew on combat missions, and was on a ship that was torpedoed. She was with the troops that liberated the concentration camp at Buchenwald,

A young woman, known as "Queenie," was one of the millions of women who went to work in a defense factory during World War II. She was photographed in front of a recruitment poster during her training at Bethune-Cookman College, Daytona Beach, Florida. (Library of Congress)

Germany. Her photographs and articles appeared in *Life* magazine and in numerous books.

The war ended in 1945, and postwar America became a very different place for women. Returning servicemen reclaimed many of the jobs that women had done during the war. Throughout the late 1940s and 1950s, the media and advertising bombarded women with the message that a "normal" woman fulfilled herself by baking, sweeping, and tending to the needs of her husband and children. Record numbers of women got married. They had so many babies, they produced what is known as the "baby boom." Suburbs mushroomed across the country, and many married women found themselves living in isolated tracts of identical-looking houses on the outskirts of cities and towns.

Despite the hype about the domestic life, the number of women in the workforce continued to increase. Most women worked in order to survive. Other women worked to help support the consumer lifestyle that Americans were eagerly embracing. Some women who did not have a financial need worked anyhow because they wanted the challenge, stimulation, and sense of meaning that work can bring.

As for the popular standard of female beauty during this time, voluptuous movie stars such as Jayne Mansfield and Marilyn Monroe were widely popular, and suddenly big busts were the rage. Advertisers pushed bust-enhancing exercise programs and creams. Department stores opened specialty shops with "trained fitters" to sell an array of bras, including padded bras. Many women who grew up in the 1950s repeated the refrain, "I must, I must, I must, I must develop my bust."

The 1950s were not a particularly progressive time for women. Nevertheless, women continued to make advances. Daisy Bates, Ella Baker, Jo Ann Robinson, and Rosa Parks challenged the rampant racial segregation and discrimination that existed in America. Mary Velasquez Riley was the first woman elected to the Apache Tribal Council. Mary Bunting devoted her career as a scientist and educator to changing "the climate of unexpectation" concerning women's intellectual abilities. Willie Mae Thornton's recording of "Hound Dog" reached number one on the rhythm and blues (R&B) chart, three years before Elvis Presley recorded the same song. Ruth Brown became one of the first R&B singers to cross over to the pop charts with hits such as "Tweedle Dee," "Bop Ting-a-Ling," "Fee Fi Fo Fum," and "Jim Dandy Got Married."

The 1960s were a time of intense questioning and change in America. Young people, some of whom were called "hippies," created a counterculture. Music was a central part of it, in particular folk music, which often pointed out the injustice and hypocrisy in society. Some young people embraced rock music and used psychedelic drugs. Many rejected the prevailing conventions of society, including monogamy and the consumer lifestyle.

The civil rights movement grew in intensity, and women such as Fannie Lou Hamer and Diane Nash played important roles in it. "The movement had a way of reaching inside you and bringing out things that even you didn't know were there. Such as courage. When it was time to go to jail, I was much too busy to be afraid," Nash later recalled. New issues emerged, including the modern environmental crusade that was energized by Rachel Carson's book, *Silent Spring,* in which she warned about the dangers of insecticides to the environment.

By the mid-1960s, protests against the Vietnam War were spreading across America. Groups of Native Americans were seeking justice. Mexican-American farmworkers were protesting horrendous working conditions. Dolores Huerta, a cofounder of the United Farm Workers Union, organized strikes, led boycotts, and marched in support of various causes including pro-choice, or the legal right of women to have an abortion. Huerta was arrested at least twenty-two times. On one occasion, she was beaten unconscious by a police officer. "One thing I've learned as an organizer and activist," she said of her experiences, "is that [you] . . . strengthen your emotional, spiritual, activist muscles."

In 1963, two events happened that helped spark what is known as the modern-day women's movement. The Presidential Commission on the Status of Women, the first ever appointed, released a report that documented the difficulties and discrimination that women faced. That same year, Betty Friedan published *The Feminine Mystique,* in which she criticized the idea that marriage and motherhood were all that women needed to lead fulfilling lives. Friedan condemned the role the media played in promoting one-dimensional images of women. She urged women to "stop giving lip service to the idea that there are no battles left to be fought for women in America."

During the 1960s, new organizations were formed, including the National Organization for Women. Congress passed the Civil Rights Act of 1964, which banned sex discrimination in employment. The words "feminism" and "feminist," which had been used during the first part of the century, reappeared. According to the writer Rebecca West, "I have never been able to find out precisely what feminism is: I only know that people call me a feminist whenever I express sentiments that differentiate me from a doormat." New words were coined such as "sexism" and "sexist." The latter, according to one definition, is someone "who proclaims or justifies or assumes the supremacy of one sex (guess which) over the other."

Alice Walker introduced the word "womanist" and defined it as: "A black feminist or feminist of color. From the black folk expression of mothers to female children, 'You acting womanish,' i.e., like a woman. . . . Responsible. In charge. *Serious*." Women also called themselves "women's liberationists," which was typically shortened to "women's libbers," especially by critics. The term "consciousness-raising groups" was coined to refer to weekly meetings in which women talked about their experiences as women in society.

On August 26, 1970—the fiftieth anniversary of winning the vote—thousands of women throughout America took part in the Women's Strike for Equality. There were parades, pickets, rallies, and teach-ins. In New York City, thousands of women marched down Fifth Avenue. Police on horseback tried to keep the women on the sidewalks because the city had refused to close off Fifth Avenue to traffic. "But there were so many women," Betty Friedan later wrote. "I was walking with Judge Dorothy Kenyon, who in her eighties refused to ride in the car we'd provided . . . , and one young radical in blue jeans. I took their hands and said to the women on each side, *take hands and stretch across the whole street*. And so we marched, in great swinging long lines, from sidewalk to sidewalk, and the police on their horses got out of our way."

The 1970s were exhilarating times for many women. Consciousness-raising groups proliferated. Women filed and won some sex discrimination suits against federal agencies, businesses, and universities. Court decisions struck down some discriminatory laws. The U.S. Supreme Court handed down a ruling that protected a woman's right to end a pregnancy. Many new laws were passed, including Title IX of the Higher Education Act which prohibited schools from spending more money on athletics for men and boys, a practice that was widespread. There was a flurry of firsts in every aspect of American life: first female network news anchor, first woman FBI agent, first woman Episcopal priest and Jewish rabbi, first regularly scheduled woman commercial airline pilot, first woman to run officially in the Boston Marathon, first woman member of the New York Stock Exchange, and the first woman to play in the U.S. Marine Corps band.

As had been true throughout American history, these advances for women were hotly debated. By the mid-1970s, groups such as the Eagle Forum and Moral Majority zeroed in on stopping the women's movement because they saw it as a threat to the traditional family. In particular, they targeted the pending Equal Rights Amendment (ERA), which read, "Equality of rights under the law shall not be denied or abridged by the United States or by any State on account of sex." Congress had passed the ERA. But before it became the law of the land, thirty-eight states needed to ratify it by June 30, 1982. The opposition launched a fierce attack that included telling people that the ERA meant unisex toilets and women in military combat. When the deadline arrived, the ERA was defeated, three states short.

During the 1980s, critics of the women's movement were effective in slowing down, and even setting back, progress in some areas. But many women kept forging ahead, including a young performer named Madonna, who was born Madonna Louise Veronica Ciccone. She burst into the popular culture the same year that the ERA was defeated. From the start, Madonna was controversial because she challenged the conventional ideas about how women performers should act and look, especially in the area of sexuality. A firestorm of debates about her appearance, behavior, and music swirled around her as she soared to stardom. Unfazed, Madonna said, "I may be dressing like the typical bimbo, but I'm in charge . . . doing the things I want to do, making my own decisions." Other independent women songwriters and performers included Laurie Anderson, Tracy Chapman, and Queen Latifah. Through their music, they spoke out about many issues, including sexism, racism, homophobia, substance abuse, homelessness, censorship, and acquired immunodeficiency syndrome, or AIDS.

By the end of the 1980s, Sally Ride had become the first American woman to fly into outer space. Wilma Mankiller had been elected the first female chief of the Cherokee Nation. And Toni Morrison had won the prestigious Pultizer Prize for her book *Beloved*. Women made up almost half of the workforce, or double the rate at the beginning of the century. The number of women lawyers and judges had increased from six percent in 1970 to twenty-seven percent, the number of physicians from eleven percent to twenty-two percent, and the number of stockbrokers from thirteen percent to thirty percent. From 1980 to 1990, the number of women stand-up comedians increased from two percent to twenty percent.

During the 1990s, many rights and freedoms that women had fought hard for were taken for granted, including the vote, an education, access to birth control, broad occupational opportunities, and comfortable clothes. However, there were many things that women could not take for granted, such as freedom from sexual harassment, domestic violence, and sexual assault; equal opportunity for career advancement and equal pay; and affordable, high quality health care and child care.

Throughout the 1990s, women tackled these issues, often using the rapidly developing computer technology to communicate and set up Web sites. One of the most comprehensive is http://www.feminist.org/. This site offers everything from action alerts on political, medical, and cultural issues and a research center to feminist reviews of films and mystery books. It has links to many other sites. Another site, http://www.nwhp.org/ is a clearinghouse for multicultural women's history resources and offers program ideas for students, teachers, and librarians.

Although no one knows what the next century will bring, the legacy of the twentieth century is clear: American women have proven over and over again that they are determined to be full participants in every aspect of life. As the twenty-first century unfolds, women will undoubtedly face future challenges with creativity and courage as they continue to play key roles in shaping American society.

Penny Colman is the widely published, award-winning author of articles, essays, stories, and books for all ages. She is also known for her photography and picture research, which are featured in her most recent book, *Corpses, Coffins, and Crypts: A History of Burial.* Her other works include *Rosie the Riveter: Women Working on the Home Front in World War II; Spies! Women in the Civil War; Madam C. J. Walker: Building a Business Empire; Breaking the Chains: The Crusade of Dorothea Lynde Dix; Fannie Lou Hamer and the Fight for the Vote; Mother Jones and the March of the Mill Children;* and *A Woman Unafraid: The Achievements of Frances Perkins.*

THE CHANGING CONCEPT OF CIVIL RIGHTS IN AMERICA

Washington, D.C., August 28, 1963. The summer sun glimmered on the reflecting pool in front of the Lincoln Memorial. Hundreds of buses had poured into the nation's capital from across the country. The travelers to Washington on that bright Wednesday came with a single purpose: to support the civil rights movement. Hundreds of thousands of people, white and black, many from other countries, had banded together to march on the capital in a stirring demonstration of their belief that equality for all was the ideal that the entire world should embrace.

The atmosphere was a happy one; the *New York Times* described it as being like "a huge picnic." Speeches were made, songs were sung, black and white leaders were interviewed by the media, prayers were offered for peace and the promise of justice. The culminating moment, however, came when a thirty-four-year-old minister from Atlanta, Georgia, Martin Luther King, Jr., stepped to the podium.

"I have a dream," King said, "that my four children will one day live in a nation where they will not be judged by the color of their skin but by the content of their character."

It was a stirring speech and, for the United States, a defining moment in the annals of civil rights. The country had made a statement to itself and to the world that a great many of its peoples were determined to bring equality to all of its peoples, to rely upon the content of individual character rather than the color of one's skin. It did not mean, for African Americans, that the struggle for equality was over, or even nearly so, but it did mean that America had openly declared that equality for all under the law was the right thing for which to strive.

There have been many grand documents created throughout the history of mankind to insure justice within a given population. Many read well, some are exciting, most at least suggest a basic fairness. But the true worth of any body of laws lies not in its language, but in how the citizens of a given country define themselves in relationship to the laws. Do they intend to enforce the laws? Do they think that the protections provided by the laws are binding even for those whom they don't like?

Throughout our history, the Constitution of the United States has been the guidepost that American citizens, great and small, have turned to as the bedrock of our democracy. It is this document, which represents the feelings and ideals of the people, that has helped bring to African Americans the opportunity to fully enjoy the fruits of this

Martin Luther King, Jr., at March on Washington, expressed his idea of a democracy in which all Americans would be judged not by the color of their skin but by the content of their character. (UPI/Corbis Bettman)

society. The journey from having been enslaved in America to the March on Washington in 1963 was a long and arduous one.

African Americans were first introduced to this country as part of the slave trade from 1619 through 1807. As slaves, they were denied most human and civil rights. When the rebellious English colonies officially became a country after the Revolutionary War, the status of most blacks did not change. Some blacks at the end of the war had acquired their freedom, but the vast majority, even some of those who had helped to defeat the British, had not. The Constitution was created by men who were determined to establish independence from Great Britain but who also recognized the existence of slavery in their own country. The words "slaves" and "slavery" were never specifically mentioned in the Constitution, but it was understood that slavery was allowed in the new United States simply because it was not specifically forbidden.

The struggle for civil rights during the period of slavery took several forms. The slaves sought to increase their rights by controlling the one thing they possessed, their own persons. Denying their service by escaping was an effective means of protest. Many slaves managed to escape from the Southern states, where slavery was widespread, and find their freedom in the North. Masters had to consider how they treated their slaves if they did not want them to run away. There were also rebellions, many of them bloody. In 1831, Nat Turner led a group of slaves in a rebellion in Virginia that took the lives of dozens of whites.

Whites who opposed slavery during this period applied to the courts and to constitutional protections. The results of these legal cases sometimes worked against blacks. An important example of this was the legal case of Dred Scott, heard before the Supreme Court in 1857. In this case, a lawsuit was brought before the Court stating that Scott was no longer a slave because he had been taken into a territory in which slavery had been barred by the federal government. The Supreme Court's ruling was a devastating one. It said that the federal government, under the Constitution, did not have the power to limit slavery in the newly acquired territories of the West. It also said that, since there was slavery when the Constitution was ratified, the protections of the Constitution could not have included blacks. In short, blacks had no rights under the Constitution.

The Civil War effectively put an end to slavery in the United States, and shortly after the war, Congress passed the Thirteenth Amendment which specifically outlawed slavery. Next, the Fourteenth Amendment, stated that all persons born in the United States were citizens and entitled to the rights of citizenship. Then, the Fifteenth Amendment said that the right to vote could not be abridged by the federal government or any state because of race, color, or previous condition of servitude.

But these amendments, which seem on their face to ensure equality to all American citizens, were full of problems. For example, while the Fifteenth Amendment stated that no citizen could be denied the right to vote because of race or color or because he had once been enslaved, it did not guarantee the right to vote. Nor did it extend the right to vote to women. In response to it, some southern states imposed a poll tax that each person had to pay in order to vote. This tax was high enough to prevent many poor blacks from voting. Literacy tests were also used to deny blacks the right to vote. African Americans, now established as citizens by constitutional amendment, still found themselves trying to participate fully in American life.

In 1896, Homer Adolph Plessy, a black passenger on a train, refused to move to the section of the train reserved for black passengers. In Louisiana, where the incident occurred, there were laws (called "Jim Crow laws") that stated that blacks were restricted to riding in those areas designated for them. Mr. Plessy was arrested and the case brought to court. Eventually, it was appealed all the way up to the Supreme Court, the highest court in the United States. The Supreme Court upheld the laws of Louisiana. It was not a violation of the Constitution, the Court said, if the facilities for blacks were "equal" to those of whites. This case, commonly referred to by the title on the court papers, *Plessy v. Ferguson,* became the basis of segregation.

To African Americans, the "separate but equal" doctrine meant that they were second-class citizens. The simple truth was that the "equal" part of the ruling was never truly equal in fact. Those people who wanted to establish white dominance over blacks used segregation to exclude them from institutions of higher learning, hospitals, toilet facilities, hotels, swimming pools, and wherever else they chose. Often, theaters had "colored" sections. In many parts of the South, blacks had to sit in the rear of buses and often had to surrender their seats to any white persons who wanted them. African Americans had the enormous burden of proving that facilities were not, in fact, equal when on paper they might appear so. The courts offered little help in this area.

Beyond the idea that the opportunities afforded to African Americans were limited, there was also a psychological burden to bear. Being denied the right even to drink from a public fountain or sit in a waiting room in a train station simply because of the color of one's skin created feelings of inferiority. A black person, without regard to his or her character or ability to pay, could not eat in a "white-only" restaurant in the South simply because of skin color.

In the first half of the twentieth century, the black struggle for civil rights—often aided by sympathetic whites—had two major goals: to protest the treatment of African Americans and to convince whites that blacks were deserving of equality.

When individuals or a mob take justice into their own hands, denying an accused person the right of a trial, it is called "lynching." Lynching can result in the hanging, shooting, or beating of the accused by people who do not have the legal authority to do so. At the turn of the century, African Americans were being lynched at an alarming rate. While the actual lynchers were usually depicted as unruly mobs led by poor, uneducated whites, lynching happened mostly because it was condoned by the affluent, well-educated people who profited most by keeping African Americans in a position of second-class citizenship.

Segregation and the denial of opportunities for blacks had created a class of people who were forced to take the leavings of the white majority. Since the turn of the century found most black Americans living in the South, where segregation was the most virulent, it also found most blacks living in a society in which they could not compete on an equal basis. To be white was always to have an advantage over being nonwhite.

The National Association for the Advancement of Colored People

(NAACP) was formed to protest the treatment of black Americans. Marches were held decrying lynching, and articles of protest were written. These were largely ineffective because the reasons for denying blacks equal rights had nothing to do with what was right or wrong. It had everything to do with the economic and social advantages that were gained by relegating people to a legally inferior position.

Black thinkers and artists made a strong effort to influence the white majority (blacks in the first half of the century represented between twelve and fifteen percent of the total population). Among these black intellectuals were scholars such as Alain Locke and W.E.B. Du Bois, writers such as Zora Neale Hurston and Countee Cullen, and scientists such as George Washington Carver and Dr. Daniel Hale Williams.

But the narrow interpretation of the Constitution, along with the reluctance of a majority of white Americans to get actively involved in the quest for civil rights, prevented any great gains for the mass of black Americans through the 1930s.

The National Association for the Advancement of Colored People was formed to study ways that African Americans could secure equal rights. (Ethrac Publications)

The tide began to turn in the 1940s as the result of a number of factors. One very strong factor was the accumulation of wealth in the African-American community. Another, important consideration was the development of mass communication via radio and, later, television.

Between 1900 and the Great Depression of 1929, most African Americans had been involved in agricultural work or low-paying laboring jobs. But during the twenties and thirties, a great many blacks moved north to the more industrialized areas of the country. During World War II, blacks found jobs in the huge defense industry in which they were generally paid as well as whites.

When the war ended in 1945 with victories over Germany and Japan, a jubilant nation demanded the consumer goods they had been denied during the war years. The economy of the nation boomed, and so did that of blacks. Production techniques learned during the war brought toasters, television sets, vacuum cleaners, and a host of other household items into the range of the average citizen and swelled the American economy. Blacks became both earners and consumers. A new sense of optimism was developing in the black community, and it reached a high point in 1948.

Blacks had served well in the armed forces during the wartime struggle against Germany and Japan, and there was a sense of pride within the black community. A. Philip Randolph, who had organized the Brotherhood of Sleeping Car Porters in 1925, pushed the president, Harry S. Truman, to integrate the armed forces. Truman, a southerner, had shown sympathies toward blacks in the past. He had helped create the group of black fliers known as the Tuskegee Airmen who had fought so well in the Army Air Force. Truman first appointed a commission to study the issue and then, in spite of very strong opposition, ordered the armed forces to integrate in 1948. This, coupled with the fact that a black baseball player, Jackie Robinson, had been accepted into the major leagues the previous year, gave blacks the feeling that maybe, at last, they would take their rightful place as Americans who had helped to build and defend a nation.

Their optimism was dashed, however, as southern congressmen fought to maintain the status quo. Any legislative acts that appeared

The forming of the Tuskegee Airmen was a quiet victory for civil rights during World War II. (National Archives)

to help blacks were met with legal maneuvers to stop them.

But the accumulation of wealth within the black community presented the opportunity for a new form of protest, the boycott. In New York City, a young minister named Adam Clayton Powell Jr. threatened that blacks would not patronize any stores in Harlem in which they were not employed as equals. It didn't take long before stores that had never hired a black salesclerk were advertising for help in the *Amsterdam News,* a black paper.

White businesses in the north began to ease the informal restrictions against blacks as they tried to attract and retain the dollars spent by black consumers. These were not the first economic boycotts conducted by blacks, but the boycotts of the forties represented a more important share of the available dollars. However, boycotts worked only with businesses that were dependent on the money that blacks spent on their products.

In the 1950s, blacks tried another tack to advance their cause. *Plessy v. Ferguson* had said that separate but equal was within the boundaries of the Constitution. Suppose it could be shown that separate, in some cases, was inherently *unequal?* The first major attempt to prove this point came in the field of education.

"I just wanted to go to school with my friends," said Linda Brown, whose name is usually associated with the famous school desegregation case, *Brown v. Board of Education of Topeka.* It was the contention of the NAACP Legal Defense Fund, which supported the case all the way to the Supreme Court in 1954, that segregation in the schools was not constitutional because it caused feelings of inferiority in the children, which affected their ability to learn. In May 1954, the high court agreed. School segregation was officially ended.

The headlines in the black community were jubilant but cautious. How would the South react? While many whites welcomed the ruling that would allow the South to shed the stigma of being bigoted and backward, traditions die hard. Southern segregationists were defiant, and within months, the nation was seeing images of black children being escorted into previously all-white schools by National Guardmen while jeering mobs screamed epithets. Court-ordered integration could not change people's hearts and minds.

But because of the Supreme Court's decision, what would have remained a local issue in the twenties and thirties now became a national issue. And what would have been merely local incidents of whites verbally abusing black children were transformed into a national and worldwide issue when television news shows broadcast the incidents throughout the country.

Slowly, surely, the schools began to integrate.

But if school integration was a major step forward for blacks, it was a call to arms for those interested in maintaining a segregated nation.

The 1960s found blacks using three potent strategies against the segregationists. Lawyers continued to challenge the meaning of equality in the courts. In some places, economic boycotts produced negotiations rather than confrontations. And where once Americans could believe that segregation was a relatively harmless policy, the nonviolent protest movement, led by Martin Luther King, Jr., exposed its brutality and inhumanity.

For a people bereft of their civil rights there is a constant threat of

Peaceful protests, such as this demonstration against segregated dining facilities, were typical of Martin Luther King, Jr.'s nonviolent approach to civil rights. (Archives of Labor and Urban Affairs, Wayne State University)

violence. This was the reality that appeared night after night on American television as praying children were set upon by police dogs and middle-aged black women were beaten in the streets. While whites had always been involved in the civil rights struggle, the media coverage that exposed the ugly injustice of racism brought many more northern and southern whites into the movement. The primary players, though; were those blacks who were willing to stand up for what they believed in when to do so meant to endanger their very lives. Two men stood out as willing to make this sacrifice: Martin Luther King, Jr. and Malcolm X.

Martin Luther King, Jr. (1929–1968) was a young minister when he was asked to be a spokesperson for the bus boycott in Montgomery, Alabama. Rosa Parks, a seamstress long active in the civil rights movement, had refused to give up her seat and move to the rear of a bus when told to do so by a white bus driver. In Montgomery, as in other parts of the South, it was the law that blacks had to move when there were no seats left in the front of the bus for whites. Rosa Parks was arrested and faced with a fine. The black citizens in Montgomery, led by the local NAACP, decided to protest by boycotting the bus company. Black ministers have always served as leaders in their communities, so it was no surprise that King was chosen to speak for the boycotters to both the local authorities and the press.

King represented a strategy that was well thought out and right for its time. It was an extension of the idea that whites could be persuaded to grant blacks equal rights through logic and peaceful demonstrations. Wouldn't it be logical if the bus company stopped making blacks give up their seats in order to keep them riding the buses in Montgomery?

The nonviolent aspect of King's movement also attracted the sympathy of the nation. Here was a peaceful man of God being attacked by savage racists. In the court of world opinion, King was winning the struggle. In the streets of the South, still controlled by an errant tradition, he was barely holding his own.

As the world watched, Martin Luther King, Jr. lead marches in the south, a new voice was being heard in the North. Malcolm X (1925–1965) had been a small-time criminal, a street hustler, and had spent time in jail before joining the Nation of Islam. He came from a background similar to Martin Luther King's. Malcolm's father, like Martin's, was a minister. His mother wrote for the newspaper published by Marcus Garvey, a militant black who was active during the twenties and thirties.

But while King preached nonviolent protest in the South, Malcolm exhorted his followers to use their economic power and self-discipline to create a black nation within a nation that would not be dependent on whites. King saw integration as the creation of an ideal American society in which blacks and whites would be equal and judged only by the "content of their

Malcolm X, a fiery speaker, offered a different philosophy for the civil rights movement. He questioned the possibility of a nonviolent revolution. (Ethrac Publications)

character." Malcolm saw an integrated country as a society ruled by white majority interest in which the blacks would always be inferior.

Malcolm X also brought a new element into the civil rights struggle. Whereas the major movement of the 1960s was led by King and represented the black middle class, Malcolm appealed directly to the poorer, working-class blacks, urging them not only to participate in the movement but to take the initiative in it. And while the movement was nonviolent in the South, Malcolm did not rule out violence. He wanted to achieve civil rights for blacks "by any means necessary."

During their brief lives (both King and Malcolm were assassinated at the age of thirty-nine) it was King's philosophy that prevailed. Under King's leadership, America—including most southerners— became outraged and ashamed as the civil rights struggles exploded into their living rooms with the six o'clock news. More and more people began to support the protesters. This swell of support reached its climax in the March on Washington in August 1963, when Martin Luther King delivered his historic "I Have a Dream" speech.

A month later, in Birmingham, Alabama, a black church was bombed. Four little girls were killed. The struggle had not ended.

But the move toward civil rights had gained a momentum that would not be stopped. There would still be struggles, and there would still be outrages visited upon people striving to enter the ranks of first-class citizenship. Racism and de facto segregation still exist in the United States. There are still people who would deny blacks, homosexuals, women, and other groups the rights implied by the Constitution.

During the 1980s and 1990s, the push toward civil rights took a peripheral role in American society. Some people believe that there is no longer a need to protest apparent wrongs. The conservative right suggests that the efforts to bring equality to all Americans, such as affirmative action, have gone too far. However, there can be no dispute that the civil rights movement in this country needs to be studied and understood.

From the beginning, the movement was an effort to ensure that all Americans would receive the protections and rights guaranteed to them by the Constitution, and would be able to live freely and fully, whatever their race or religion. But while America is a land of opportunity, that opportunity is not without qualification and responsibilities. The civil rights of individuals are effective only inasmuch as individuals are prepared through education and good citizenship to take advantage of them. Civil rights are eroded when they are not used. In communities in which participation in the voting process is minimal and in which educational standards are allowed to deteriorate, what we know as civil rights can be effectively surrendered.

For African Americans, the movement from slavery to segregation to a society largely integrated and free of legal impediments has been a triumph of democracy. That is not to say that the struggle has been totally won or that those rights won do not have to be diligently protected. The present challenge, a formidable one, will be for all Americans to secure a full measure of civil rights by exercising the right to vote and by preparing themselves, through education and attentiveness, to seize the opportunities that are the fruits of liberty.

Brave men and women before us have sacrificed much to bring these rights within our reach. It is up to us now, as Americans of all races, to fulfill the dream of the Constitution: that the equality of all people will be forever self-evident.

––––––––––

Walter Dean Myers identifies himself as one who has survived long enough to have known a grandfather born in slavery (his mother received documentation from the plantation house recording his birth in 1860s Virginia) and a son who attended the college (Brown University) that was created by a fortune made from the profits of the slave trade. Mr. Myers says it has been an exciting journey. His most recent books are *At Her Majesty's Request: An African Princess in Victorian England; Monster;* and *The Journal of Joshua Loper: Black Cowboy.*

FASHIONING OURSELVES

Photographs were very much part of our household, of our lives. My grandmother's sister became a photographer not long after the turn of the century. My own father, every time we moved—and we moved often—always pointed to a room and announced, "Darkroom" before we children had a chance to stake out our own territories. And in my thirties, I dismantled an entire basement room, ripping out the shelves intended for storage of canned homegrown produce, to create space for my enlarger and bottles of chemicals.

Our lives were documented for generations. So were our clothes, our hairstyles, all the ways in which we continually reinvented ourselves, thinking we were so hip, so cool, so with-it, and so entitled to thumb our noses at everyone who came before.

Across my long tabletop of desk, I have lined them up: six generations. Kate. Helen. The next Kate. Me. Then my daughter, Alix (who, re-creating herself in the 1980s, changed her name to Max). And finally Nadine, my grandaughter, usually called Bean, who is celebrating her fifth birthday as I write these words.

The first Kate, my great-grandmother, was born in 1845 and was fifteen in the photograph I have of her, taken in Cincinnati the year that the Civil War began. We all know those years, and their fashions, because of *Gone with the Wind;* we remember the early scene in which Scarlett urges her maid to pull the corset strings tighter so that her waist will be the smallest at the party.

Judging from the photo, Kate Gordon would not have played Scarlett in the movie. She would have been Melanie, played by Olivia De Havilland, the unflamboyant one with a sweet face and solemn eyes. Kate's twin sister, Anna, is dressed identically and equally solemnly in a separate portrait; the twins' hair is parted in the middle and pulled neatly back. They look not so much like teenagers as staid housewives, even at fifteen (though Kate didn't marry until she was thirty-one, and Anna never married at all).

Kate at fifteen

It is clear that their family is well-to-do; the fabric of the dresses is richly embroidered and bordered with what appears to be velvet. The laundering would have required servants.

I remember Kate, my great-grandmother, though she died at ninety-six when I was only four. My sister and I called her Nanny and were taken to visit her, wearing hand-smocked dresses instead of our usual corduroy overalls. We didn't care what we wore. But I remember that it was important to Mother, that she cautioned us not to play boisterously on the grass, which would cause green immutable stains on our pink dresses, and that she tied and retied our sashes and straightened our short white socks before we were led in to kiss Nanny on the cheek.

My great-grandmother had diamond earrings, a wedding gift from her husband, with special gold coverings like caps that she wore over them in daytime, revealing the gems only in the evening, when adornment was considered more proper. When she was widowed, Kate removed the earrings, deeming them an unseemly display. (Today, I wear one of Kate's diamonds, made into a ring; my daughter-in-law, Margret, wears the other.)

Helen at sixteen

Though she married late (and had probably been thought a spinster), Kate Gordon had five children; the oldest was my grandmother, Helen Rebecca, whose photographs are here in front of me, too. At sixteen, her waist is as tiny as Scarlett O' Hara's. Her white high-necked dress is intricately tucked and ruffled. (I can see, in my imagination, a basement scullery, with laundresses hard at work daily, their hands raw from harsh soaps. Kate had four daughters, each of them beautifully clothed; even her youngest child, the only son, wore starched white sailor suits.)

Helen at twenty

Helen's hair is more luxuriant than her mother's, and more abundantly displayed, pulled up in a wavy pompadour and adorned with a huge and frivolous hair ribbon that perches atop like a bird about to take flight.

Four years later, graduating from college in 1897, she is more subdued, dressed sternly in an academic robe and a high starched collar, her hair unwaved. *I am here to take my place in the world,* the proud and solemn expression of this well-educated young woman says.

Three years later, as the century turns—and she has a suitor, a young banker—Helen is photographed again. Now she wears lavish lace, and her hair is piled again in feminine waves.

Helen at twenty-three

Whatever aspirations she had as that young academic are in the past now. "Her only ornament," the 1905 Cincinnati newspaper says of the bride, after describing her gown (white panne crepe trimmed with point d'Alençon), "was an exquisite double crescent of pearls and diamonds, the gift of the groom." Her father, General Joseph Boyd, had adorned her mother with diamond earrings. Now Helen's groom decorates her, staking his claim with jewels.

She takes her place at her husband's side, bearing his children and supervising the seamstress and laundress who will stitch and tend their fragile embroidered baby garments. My mother, the second Kate, was born in 1906 and photographed throughout her childhood wearing hand-smocked, lace-trimmed dresses. Looking at the photographs, I again remember my mother, thirty-five years later, dressing my sister and me for visits to our great grandmother. When she set aside our sturdy play clothes and buttoned and primped us into such splendor, she was re-creating herself as a child.

Photographed at ten, Kate had waist-long hair. But here is Kate at eighteen in the 1920s. Demure and dressed conservatively, with pearls at her throat, nonetheless her hair has been cut short. I remember my mother telling me the story of her haircut, her first rebellious act.

"All the girls were doing it," my mother told me, remembering. "But my mother was absolutely furious. Livid."

I picture the banker's wife, wearing her pearl-and-diamond crescent, fluttering her gloved hand in front of her face, perhaps threatening to faint, at the sight of her daughter's bobbed hair. I picture her reacting to the timeworn rationalization: "All my friends are doing it."

My memory fast-forwards to the 1950s. My mother, Kate, is now a dentist's wife (no newspaper records a groom's gift of jewels). I am her second daughter. I am seventeen. My photo at this age shows me long-haired, well combed, wearing white gloves and a string of pearls. My shoulders are bare in a way that would have seemed shockingly inappropriate to my grandmother.

Kate at ten

Kate at eighteen

Lois at seventeen

A college freshman, I envied some of my classmates and friends who were to be presented to society at a formal ball during Christmas vacation. They were spending a lot of time choosing finery.

"I wish I could have a coming out party," I whined to my parents when I was home for Thanksgiving. "All my friends are."

"You came out seventeen years ago," my father told me.

"Weighing seven pounds ten ounces," my mother added.

"You're as out as you're ever going to be," Dad concluded, and so went my dreams of a white ball gown and elbow-length gloves.

Sulkily, I took the kitchen scissors and chopped off my long hair. I bought a man's trench coat at a military surplus store and wore it everywhere I went. I began to smoke Marlboros. If I couldn't be a debutante, I would be a Bohemian.

My mother didn't call for smelling salts. She simply rolled her eyes.

But no photographs exist of me in my short-lived Bohemian persona. My father, an inveterate photographer with several Leicas always at the ready, said he'd be damned if he was going to record his daughter looking like a Singapore slut.

My parents' marriage in the 1930s came at a time when fashion would soon change abruptly because of war. My mother, still short-haired but no longer the rebellious flapper of the twenties, brought to her marriage a trousseau of elegant dresses made by hand by her mother's seamstress; but she entered a life that no longer included household staff. There was an Asian nursemaid when I was born in 1937—she appears in a few photographs, holding me—but World War II put an end to all of that. Women went to well-paid work in factories and were no longer willing to do other women's laundry.

My father went overseas and my mother took us home to her parents' house; but there was no longer a staff of servants there, either: just the cook, who grumbled that I was underfoot in the kitchen. Great-grandmother—Nanny—died; her diamond earrings went into a safe-deposit box and were virtually forgotten. There were no more formal dinner parties. Instead, there was the seven o'clock news on the big radio in Grandfather's library and a Bendix washing machine installed in the darkest corner of the basement, near the coal furnace.

Some of my mother's friends, young women her age, began to wear slacks. It was slightly shocking to me, as a child, to see women in trousers for the first time.

"She's divorced," my mother whispered to me of a woman she knew. I was ten and felt quite mature to have such shocking knowledge. Mother took my sister Helen and me to see *Gone With the Wind* and we watched, trembling with passion, as Scarlett made a fancy gown from the draperies and swore never to be hungry (or badly dressed) again.

Helen and I played endlessly with movie-star paper dolls. We cut out clothes for June Allyson and Susan Hayward, then we traced their outlines on typing paper and designed new ones for them, carefully coloring with our Crayolas.

"This is June's beach outfit," I would say, showing my sister the bright flowered shorts and halter with a matching beach coat I had designed.

"Here's the dress she wears to cocktails with Dick Powell," Helen would say, laboriously drawing gold buttons down the front of a blue midcalf-length dress.

Our taste was defined by Hollywood in the forties, and we deemed our own mother tragically deficient in her lack of sequins, platform shoes, or fur jackets. My sixth-grade class, lined up for a photograph in 1947, shows eleven little girls, each wearing a dress and neatly folded ankle socks. Each of us was harboring a fantasy in which we would magically be catapulted to California, where we would acquire strapless gowns with billowy tulle skirts.

But Hollywood had been affecting us for decades. My mother, bobbing her hair as a teenager, also bound and clothed herself into a lanky, boyish figure, imitating the 1920s movie flappers like Clara Bow. Later, in the 1940s, she wore shoulder-padded dresses and crimson lipstick: Joan Crawford as Mildred Pierce.

My teenaged friends and I, thinking ourselves original, also fashioned ourselves according to the movies, wearing pointed bras

Lois's sixth-grade class. She is in the front row, third from the left.

(Hollywood had brought cleavage into fashion) and three-inch heels that transformed us—or so we hoped—into temptresses like Lauren Bacall while our mothers wrung their hands in dismay.

When my mother was quite literally on her deathbed, in 1992, I felt the need to apologize to her for something I had said in 1949, when I was twelve years old.

She had been in her bedroom early that evening, dressing to attend some mother-and-daughter event with me. I was already ready and waiting impatiently. Finally, she emerged, wearing her best dress, smelling of perfume, still reaching up to attach an earring.

I looked at her with what can only be described—though I shudder at the memory—as disdain.

"You're not going to wear that, are you?" I asked her, in the kind of scornful voice that a seventh-grader has always been able to do so well.

Forty-three years later my mother, frail at eighty-six years old, listened from a hospital bed to my description, to my imitation of my adolescent voice, and to my apology. She began, to my surprise, to laugh.

"I don't even remember it," she told me.

"Then why are you laughing?" I asked.

"Because," my mother explained, "you sounded so much like me, talking to my mother, back in 1918. I thought she was the most old-fashioned, completely out-of-it person on the planet."

"Because of her clothes?"

Mother reflected for a moment, an oxygen tube silently providing breath in her last days. "And her hair," she remembered, chuckling.

My own daughter at seventeen hadn't the slightest desire to be introduced to society at a debutante ball. But I see so much of the past in her. At ten, long hair streaming down her back, she resembles her grandmother at the same age, though instead of a white organdy dress, she is wearing an old shirt with a visibly ripped shoulder seam.

Taken for her high school yearbook, her photograph—the same eyes as the women of each preceding generation, the same slight smile—shows her wearing jeans and a T-shirt. Her feet, not in the photograph, are bare. Forgetting the misery and discomfort of the wires and bones that shaped my teenage self, now as a mother I wished my daughter would wear a bra.

For her college graduation photograph four years later, she donned a large hat and rhinestone-trimmed sunglasses.

Alix (Max), age ten

When my granddaughter, the remarkable Bean, was almost two years old, I went to visit her and took with me a child's dress I had found in an antique shop. Probably a hundred years old, it was hand-stitched batiste, lined with tiny tucks at the yoke and decorated at the neck and cuffs with exquisite lace: almost identical to the dresses my own mother wore in toddler photographs.

Alix (Max), age seventeen

My daughter-in-law stripped Beanie out of her OshKosh overalls and put her in the antique dress. Then we took her outdoors to a nearby meadow, and I photographed her as she followed her dog through the wildflowers.

She looked like an elfin child from a bygone time, magically set down to remind us what little girls were like long ago when life had a slower pace and mothers had servants in the laundry room.

Alix (Max), age twenty-one

But Bean is scowling in all of the photographs. She lasted only ten minutes in the meadow. Then she bellowed, pulling at the dress, "Take this *off* of me!"

My daughter-in-law and I, laughing, looked down at ourselves.

We were both wearing jeans. It was 1995. Sympathetically, we freed Beanie from the discomfort of the past, despite its fragile beauty.

Bean at almost two

I photographed my granddaughter again just last month. She will soon be six. This time she was wearing clothes of her own choosing—a sweatshirt—and announced self-confidently that she felt quite beautiful, as indeed she was. She especially wanted her hands to be visible in the pictures, because she was wearing long red plastic fingernails.

"Aren't I cool?" my granddaughter asked, posing dramatically, arranging her talon-studded hands in front of her. "Like Barbie?"

I shook my head and rolled my eyes and laughed, watching the newest generation fashion itself anew, as each one has for centuries.

Lois Lowry, a grandmother who wears blue jeans instead of flowered housedresses, lives in Cambridge, Massachusetts. She likes movies, Mozart, Mexican food, dogs, and daffodils. Ms. Lowry is the author of many books for young people, including two Newbery winners, *Number the Stars* and *The Giver,* and the series of stories about Anastasia Krupnik.

Bean at five

MILTON MELTZER

POLITICS—NOT JUST FOR POLITICIANS

Politics" has come to be a dirty word in the vocabulary of many Americans. There are signs of a widespread public disgust with our political system. True, Americans are proud of living in the world's oldest continuous democracy. But as the twentieth century neared its end, it was clear that many didn't believe that "We, the people" actually ruled. They thought the individual counted for little against the overpowering influence of the wealthy. Professional politicians were running the system, and they were controlled by money, not votes.

Lobbyists had replaced elected representatives on every level—federal, state, local—as the primary influence on decision making. Lobbyists are people paid to serve the interests of pressure groups—corporations, trade and professional associations, labor unions, advocates of special causes, and foreign governments. Their function is to lobby the legislature and the bureaucracy to secure votes or actions that will advance their clients' interests.

But can we do without politics? Like it or not, it's a powerful force in determining the conditions of life. The decisions of government touch almost every aspect of everyday living. Politics is the activity by which different interests within a city, state, or nation work out compromises in proportion to their influence. It's like a marketplace where social demands are settled by negotiation. A bargain is struck

William McKinley
1897–1901
(National Archives)

among contending forces. For example, if the national Treasury shows a surplus, how should that money be used? To lower taxes? To shore up Social Security? To provide housing or medical insurance for the poor? Political decisions benefit some, hurt others. They impose costs that are heavier for some to bear, lighter for others.

Our American political system was created by the Founding Fathers when they wrote the Constitution. It was based on new principles of government voiced in the Declaration of Independence:

> We hold these truths to be self-evident, that all men are Created equal, that they are endowed by their Creator with certain unalienable rights, that among these are Life, Liberty and the pursuit of Happiness. That to secure those rights, Governments are instituted among Men, deriving their just powers from the consent of the governed.

Under the Constitution, people periodically elect a president and a Congress to serve their needs. These officials make the decisions. To prevent abuses, that power is checked by our balanced form of government and by the fact that those elected must satisfy the voters in order to remain in office. Decisions of government are made by majority vote, with provision for protection of the rights of minorities, such as African Americans, immigrants, or the disabled.

Since we are a large nation of diverse peoples and interests—many ethnic, racial, social, economic, and religious groups—public officials face competing demands. This makes conflict inevitable. Government's job is to mediate these varying demands, supposedly with the public benefit always in mind.

The result is generally a compromise, with no group getting its way completely. But is this what actually happens? To find out, we must look at what citizens want and what politicians do. Who gets what, and why? It's a complex question. For in addition to lobbyists and interest or pressure groups, politics includes political parties, elections, and laws. They're all tied together. Public policy is the outcome of their interaction. It comes down to a power struggle over demands, settled by negotiations. Groups differ over such questions as educa-

Theodore Roosevelt
1901–1909
(National Archives)

tion, jobs, wages, free trade, inflation, pollution of the environment, taxation, welfare, housing, health, civil rights, Social Security, and foreign policy.

People with the greatest power have the strength to get others to do what they wish. They have the resources for such control: the organization, the media, the technology, the skills, the jobs, the goods, and services people hope for—and the money that makes it all possible. The tobacco industry, for example, promised in 1998 to fund expensive and favorable television ads for congressmen in their home states if they voted to defeat a tobacco bill the cigarette companies opposed. The bill was killed.

At bottom, politics is agreement over what to negotiate about and how to do that bargaining. If politicians refuse to believe that some vital question can be negotiated, they risk the alternatives: revolution or civil war. An awareness of, a sensitivity to, the public interest is what keeps the political game going. The politics of a democracy requires common recognition of the need for alliances, for compromise, even for retreat.

At the opening of the twentieth century, Theodore Roosevelt ("TR") entered the White House. The modern age began with his presidency. It was a period of rapid industrialization and the building of great financial empires. TR loved power and used it as few presidents before him had done. He felt the old laws regarding the piling up of wealth and its distribution no longer fit public needs. Testing his strength, he used the Justice Department to prosecute a giant transportation monopoly—the National Securities Company—for violating the Anti-Trust Act, which regulated such monopolies. He was responding to a shift in public opinion that had begun in recent years. The suffering caused by the depression of the 1890s, rising prices brought about by the monopolies, and a steel strike broken by a powerful corporation that refused to deal with union labor, had all made people think some control over economic power was needed.

Why didn't TR ask Congress to take action? Because recent history demonstrated that conservatives beholden to big business dominated the legislature. The Congress would never take measures to control the corporations. So TR chose to tame the trusts by enforcing

William H. Taft
1909–1913
(National Archives)

Woodrow Wilson
1913–1921
(National Archives)

the existing antitrust laws. He saw federal regulation as the only practical way to tackle the problems created by the growth of monopolies.

But against the combined might of scores of giant corporations, his tiny Justice Department staff was able to accomplish very little. Roosevelt never wanted to destroy the corporations. He meant only to save "smug and stupid" tycoons from making serious mistakes.

A great influence upon government was the press. In those early years of the century, the media showed their power to make government responsive to the people's needs. Investigative journalists published many articles and books exposing what was glaringly wrong with both business and politics. They brought home to the public Standard Oil's ruthless ways, the grim conditions of African-American life, the plight of ten million Americans living below the poverty line, and the facts about how business interests and politicians connived in legislation.

The "muckrackers," as TR called those trying to expose misconduct, raised a national outcry for change. This led to the formation of a reform movement led by people called the "Progressives." Their militant pressure brought about the passage of several reform bills. But try as the Progressives might, they found the political system had a tremendous built-in inertia that resisted change. The power structure of the corporate system was never threatened by them.

Still, in those early years of the twentieth century, many gains were made for labor, chiefly at the state level. New state laws limited the length of the workday, thousands won the eight-hour day through their unions, many states set age limits and restricted hours for child labor, and workers' compensation laws provided payments for employees injured in industrial accidents.

Roosevelt himself was a great force for carrying out a badly needed conservation program. Half of America's forests had been destroyed by the time he took office, the rivers polluted and filled with silt, the land eroded, and many species of animals were on the verge of extinction.

The advances made in conservation during TR's administration did not come easily. He often tangled with Congress over policy on natural resources. Power companies, lumber firms, mine operations,

Warren G. Harding
1921–1923
(National Archives)

and ranchers lobbied against protective measures, believing they had a sacred right to exploit the country's resources. But with fervent moral appeals to the voters and clever political tactics with Congress, TR usually prevailed.

TR, like Abraham Lincoln, was an example of a president who used the authority he had to carry out what he considered his mandate to be. Presidents had used and abused those powers before TR's time, and they have continued to do so since. For the men in the White House have been all kinds—strong, weak, energetic, lazy, brilliant, stupid, bold, timid, honest, corrupt, narrow-minded, generous, humane, bigoted. Whatever their personal traits, there has been a general tendency to expand the power of the president. Partly, this has been the inevitable effect of the country's enormous growth in size and complexity. And partly, it springs from the political beliefs of the man holding office.

Remember that the president is the only national officer elected by the citizens of the whole country. No wonder some presidents assume that they hold all the power, that it's only their will that counts. When a president thinks that way, he may act like an emperor. He commands, the people obey. One president who acted that way—Richard Nixon—was forced to resign under the threat of impeachment.

One of the greatest tests American democracy has ever faced came with the onset of the Great Depression in the fall of 1929. Not that it was something new. America had already gone through seventeen or more depressions with mass unemployment. But this crisis was different. It came on harder and faster, engulfed a much larger part of the population, lasted much longer, and did far more and far worse damage than any before it.

Scarcely a year before it began, President Herbert Hoover had predicted that America was in sight of banishing poverty forever. The nation seemed to be aboard an express train rushing toward permanent prosperity. The stock market soared in the 1920s, more people were doing well and living comfortably than ever before, and business profits spiraled rapidly upward.

But a brutal fact was ignored: The majority of Americans in the

Calvin Coolidge
1923–1929
(National Archives)

Herbert C. Hoover
1929–1933
(National Archives)

twenties lived at or below a bare comfort level. Still, it was a better life than workers in other lands knew, and it was certainly better than the mean life American workers had known previously, or that from which their immigrant forebears had fled.

Then, late in October 1929, prices on the Wall Street stock market plunged sickeningly. The drop went lower and lower day after day. The Great Depression had begun. It exposed many weaknesses underlying the operation of a complex economic system. Wages and prices, trade and investment, production and consumption, machinery and manpower were not regulated by government and were thrown wildly off balance.

Within two months, several million people were out of work. Many businesses came to a dead halt. Years of joblessness, poverty, hunger, and disillusionment piled a weight of suffering on a huge part of the population. Children, youth, African Americans, farmers, the middle class—all were caught up in the whirlwind of disaster. By the spring of 1933, the unemployed numbered over fifteen million. One-fourth of the nation's families had no regular income.

And almost nobody—including the government—was willing or prepared to provide relief to them. After three years of depression, the country was drifting on a sea of doubt, uncertain where to turn, what the answers might be.

During the summer of 1932, the Republicans renominated Hoover for the presidency. To do otherwise would have been admitting their party's failure. The Democrats nominated Franklin Delano Roosevelt ("FDR"), governor of New York. When he won, overwhelmingly, and took office in March 1933, the country was close to complete breakdown. "The only thing we have to fear is fear itself," FDR said. He acted swiftly, calling Congress into special session and obtaining broad executive powers to wage war against the emergency.

In one hundred days, Congress adopted sixteen major measures at FDR's request. It was a program he called the "New Deal." Federal relief came first, to feed the hungry, and then billions of dollars were allocated to provide public works so the unemployed could at last find jobs. The program was not a socialist blueprint, but a patchwork of plans improvised for the emergency by the lawyers, econo-

Franklin D. Roosevelt
1933–1945
(National Archives)

mists, and sociologists whom the New Deal recruited for public service. Their function was to save capitalism, a goal FDR declared publicly. Nevertheless, FDR had many enemies, even among those whose businesses he was trying to save.

In the next few years, controls were devised to regulate business and finance. Labor was helped by a law to protect the right to organize, and farmers received aid in several forms. Laws for unemployment insurance, Social Security, and low-cost housing were adopted. There was even a program to provide work for unemployed artists, writers, musicians, and theater people; it brought their talents and creations to millions.

The spirit of the country changed quickly as FDR's optimistic personality reached everyone through the major devices he used to communicate with the country. One was his twice-weekly press conferences. The other was his "fireside chats," reserved for special occasions. For the first time, a president used the full political power of radio to instruct, to explain, to inspire. This is where we are, he was saying, this is where we are headed, and this is how we propose to get there.

Still, many millions continued to be jobless through the 1930s. It took the outbreak of World War II in Europe to put every employable American to work again in the booming defense industries. The engine of recovery was rearmament—for the European nations fighting the Nazi war machine, and for ourselves.

If mass unemployment and business stagnation had not been ended by the war, political upheaval of an unpredictable nature might have followed. But by the end of the war, the United States had become the strongest power in the world. President Harry S. Truman, who had succeeded in office upon the death of FDR in 1945, was assuming American leadership of the free world. When the explosion of atomic bombs over Hiroshima and Nagasaki ended World War II, the atomic age began. It was one of the most significant turns in world history.

Soon, the Soviet Union and other countries developed nuclear arsenals. And the horrifying threat of nuclear war has shadowed the world ever since, shaping American politics and business in many ways.

Before World War II, the military had played a minor role in American life. Now, with the threat of nuclear-armed Communist

Harry S. Truman
1945–1953
(National Archives)

power raised, the influence of the armed forces grew rapidly. Big business made high profits out of defense spending, as lobbyists and congressmen bargained for the allocation of huge defense funds to their districts. The ever-closer ties between the military and the arms industry alarmed President Dwight D. Eisenhower. As he left office in 1961, he warned of the dangers of what he called the new "military-industrial complex."

That complex became the largest single factor on the American economic and political landscape. Between 1946 and 1967, the federal government spent $904 billion on military power, as against $96 billion on social needs such as education, health, and welfare. The economic power of big business had great impact on the political system. Corporations and congressmen worked in close harmony, with lobbyists writing the tune.

Americans had once believed peace, not war, was the normal state of affairs. Now they were told the world was fated always to be preparing for war against the Communist menace. And with the most powerful military force in the world, the United States began to get involved in wars both large and small in all quarters of the globe. The first big one came in Korea in 1950–53. For many years after that, sizable military campaigns or paramilitary operations by the Central Intelligence Agency occurred on an average of every eighteen months. Iran, Guatemala, Indonesia, Lebanon, Laos, Cuba, the Congo, British Guiana, the Dominican Republic, and Nicaragua were all scenes of American military interventions.

And then, of course, there was the biggest one of all: Vietnam—the century's longest and most controversial war, which ended with American defeat and withdrawal.

The spread of communism in Europe and Asia in the postwar years was seen by the United States as a threat to our national security. To ferret out Communists in government ranks, President Harry S. Truman launched a federal loyalty investigation, and many states followed suit. The wave of suspicion among Americans was played upon by unscrupulous politicians, like a young first-term senator, Joseph McCarthy of Wisconsin. Led by McCarthy and others, an intense and

Dwight D. Eisenhower
1953–1961
(National Archives)

reckless assault upon the people, values, and institutions of American progressivism began. From 1946 through 1957, extreme conservatives within almost every institution attacked not only the Communist Party, but liberalism in general. And that included the tradition of New Deal reform.

As one commentator put it, "calling the opposition 'Reds' and 'Communist sympathizers' was a way of life for many conservatives during the postwar years." Fanaticism and fear took over during that decade of repression. Call it a politics of hysteria. Every branch of government—plus the schools, the churches, the mass media, the whole culture—was influenced by it.

Politicians built their careers upon the fear of Communism. Anyone who voiced dissenting views risked being labeled "subversive" and "un-American." To exercise the right to criticize, to hold unpopular beliefs, to protest, to think independently, cost many Americans their reputation and often their livelihood. Despite pleas for reason and decency by some brave public figures, fear dominated the popular mind for many years.

By 1961, when President John F. Kennedy took office, the lacerating politics of the McCarthy period had ended. A consensus was reached that the free enterprise system could create everlasting abundance. The only threat to a beneficient system came from the Cold War antagonism between the West and the Communist world. America had the resources and the will to satisfy human needs without social conflict.

Without it? How could that be, when the rich were getting richer and the poor were getting poorer? And when first in the South, and then soon in the North, the campaign for civil rights was meeting increasing and violent resistance? Kennedy moved slowly and reluctantly to pass a civil rights bill when he saw how much resistance there was to the black revolt. As time passed, the black demand was not just for legal equality in the South, but for social and economic equality everywhere.

These hard facts created a crisis for the presidencies of Kennedy, Lyndon Johnson, and Richard Nixon. At its center was a dilemma: Americans clung to the national ideal of equality, but the nation

John F. Kennedy
1961–1963
(National Archives)

Lyndon B. Johnson
1963–1969
(National Archives)

Richard M. Nixon
1969–1974
(National Archives)

was reluctant to do what was needed to achieve equality. The 1960s were marked by political assassinations coming fast upon one another. President Kennedy and his brother Robert, and leaders of the struggle for civil rights—the African Americans Medgar Evers, Martin Luther King, Jr., and Malcolm X.

When Vice President Lyndon B. Johnson became president upon the death of Kennedy, his aim, he said, was to achieve limitless social progress, to root out "poverty, disease and illiteracy," and to continue a commitment to resist communism worldwide. With his enormous political skill (compromise here, twist an arm there), Johnson pushed through Congress measures to carry out his "unconditional" War on Poverty.

The Congress passed two major civil rights acts, an economic opportunity bill, and Medicare, and it expanded budgets for elementary and secondary education. At the same time, Johnson made the fateful decision not to end the war in Vietnam, but to expand it. The two goals conflicted. The vast wealth it took to fight that remote war made it impossible to fund the extensive programs needed to lift out of poverty the forty to fifty million Americans who were poor by any standard. Unless, that is, those who exercised political power both in Congress and in the executive branch were willing to pay the level of taxes required by the "Great Society policy." And that they were not willing to do.

The election of Richard Nixon in 1968 signaled a swing to the right. The reason? A social scientist observed that in recent years, a union had developed between the central city poor (more and more African American) and the educated, economically secure, mostly white, Protestant suburbanites. But it was a union of groups that did not represent a national majority. The majority, he noted, were working Americans concerned not with the nation or the community, but with the protection of job, family, and home. They were neither rich nor poor, neither black nor radical. Nixon's victory was a populist revolt of Americans who had been elevated by prosperity to middle-class status and who had adopted conservative views. They were called the "Silent Majority."

Against the background of the riots, assassinations, and protests of the 1960s, Nixon promised to bring the nation together and to reinforce "law and order." But when he ordered massive bombing of North Vietnam, it accelerated antiwar protests. Nixon benefited from the Apollo mission moon landing, his pathbreaking visit to China, and the first strategic arms limitations agreement he negotiated with the USSR. But he saw himself as an absolute authority who could order people to commit illegal acts and then conspire to cover them up. The break-in at the Watergate office complex was only the last of his misdeeds, the one that brought ruin upon him. To escape impeachment, he became the first American president to resign from office.

Gerald R. Ford
1974–1977
(Gerald R. Ford Library)

Scarcely a dozen years later, another president, Ronald Reagan, was criticized for similar abuse of power. A film actor whose career had waned, he had become a spokesperson for corporations and for conservative causes. After serving two terms as governor of California, he won the presidency in 1980, and the Republicans made great gains in Congress. He promoted his policy of "Reaganomics," promising to cut taxes and social spending while vastly increasing the military budget. He also promised to balance the budget somehow at the same time. The result? The national debt shot sky-high.

Reagan ordered military adventures in Lebanon, Grenada, and Libya. Toward the end of his second term, his popularity was very high—until the Iran-Contra scandal hit the headlines. It involved secret arms sales and illegal actions to fund rebel Contra operations against the left-wing government of Nicaragua. The president had apparently lost control of his own officials, many of whom were forced to resign. Testifying as to his role in that affair after he left office, Reagan responded 130 times with "I don't recall" or "I don't remember." He never publicly condemned or acknowledged regret for the illegal actions of his own administration.

The election of George Bush to the presidency in 1988 was an example of how a politician's drive to win can overwhelm concern for the public good. Advertising and television experts packaged the Bush campaign to sell the candidate like any other product. Politics became performance art. Well-rehearsed little stunts like visiting a

James E. Carter
1977–1981
(National Archives)

flag factory were staged every day for a few seconds of managed impact on the nightly television news. Images and symbols became far more important than information. The failure to talk about the real issues disgusted so many that the voter turnout was the lowest in history.

Bush had the good luck while in office to see the Soviet Union crumble into smaller pieces. During his term, Bush worked with Soviet president Mikhail Gorbachev to end the nuclear arms race by signing the first nuclear arms reduction pact. His popularity grew when he ordered military action to liberate the oil-rich Kingdom of Kuwait, which had been occupied by Iraq. But the early cease-fire left the dictator Saddam Hussein still in control of Iraq.

Inflation got out of hand during the Bush years, and an economic recession set in. The president's popularity dropped off badly, and he failed to win a second term in office.

When Bill Clinton defeated Bush in 1992, he became the youngest president since Kennedy and the first Democrat in twelve years to win the White House. Considered a liberal, he hoped with the aid of a Democratic Congress to break the gridlock that had stymied progress for the past twelve years. He managed to make some gains on the foreign policy front, with Russia, the Middle East, Haiti, and North Korea.

But on the domestic side, his attempt to restructure the nation's health care system failed badly. The special prosecutor's investigation of the Whitewater land deal, which occurred when Clinton was governor of Arkansas, only made his situation worse. In 1994, the voters replaced Democrats with Republicans on all levels of government, winning control of both houses of Congress for the first time in over forty years.

Clinton moved to the right on domestic issues as he prepared to run for a second term. When the economy rebounded—with the stock market soaring, unemployment falling, and inflation held down—he was reelected easily in 1996. However, the ongoing Whitewater investigation, a highly publicized sexual harassment suit, and the indictment of several cabinet members for corruption continued to dog Clinton.

At the same time, the cuts in federal spending at the expense of the

Ronald W. Reagan
1981–1989
(Reagan Library)

poor while leaving middle-class benefits untouched, as well as legislation Clinton signed that weakened civil liberties, made it hard to distinguish the president from his opponents. In 1999, the House of Representatives impeached Clinton on charges of perjury and subordination of witnesses arising from the sexual harrassment suit, but the Senate voted to exonerate him.

Though politicians proclaimed national prosperity, with each party seeking credit for it, the truth was more complex. The rich were richer than ever. The top ten percent of the population, in the late 1990s, had wealth equal to that of the bottom ninety percent combined. And working people were losing ground year by year. About one in every four children lived in poverty in the closing years of the decade. While the employment rate was high, many jobs paid too little to lift a family out of poverty. The United States continued to have the highest rate of young-child poverty of any Western industrialized nation.

The political denial of aid to children was reflected in education. For example, per-pupil spending in California's once highly rated educational system—seventh in the nation in the mid-1960s—dropped down in three decades to forty-seventh. Half the state's 2,150 public libraries were closed during that time.

In the 1990s, while our economy was envied abroad, our political system, according to one sociologist, seemed "deader than dead." American politicians, he said, "engage in passionate quarrels over meaningless symbols but don't pass much innovative legislation."

Studies of middle-class opinion disclosed the lack of a shared sense of national purpose. People seemed to want the benefits of being American without the obligation of paying taxes or paying attention. Blaming politicians for everything wrong served as an excuse for doing nothing themselves.

Advocates of organized citizen action such as Ralph Nader noted the enormous resurgence of corporate power. Increasingly, wrote Nader, "the corporations, their lobbyists, their corporate law firms and their campaign money have taken over the government . . . grabbing off huge tax breaks . . . pillaging the taxpayer's assets."

Yet what politician campaigns today on cracking down on

George H. W. Bush
1989–1993
(George Bush Presidential Library)

corporate crime, fraud, and abuse? Noting this, many citizens do not vote because they have become cynical about politics. But sadly, when they turn cynical, they drop out of the democratic process. And only democratic action can build a happier, more prosperous society for all.

Although the media rarely reports it, millions of Americans have begun to realize that democracy is not what we have; it is what we do. They know the bad news that undermines hope—war, hunger, poverty, discrimination, crime, failing schools. But they have not given up. They protest, make demands, and, above all, they organize. They are learning how to join forces to solve problems.

They no longer believe their only responsibility is to come out and vote on election day. They understand that democracy is not simply a set of governmental institutions. If it is to work, it must be a way of life that involves us every day. Our private life cannot be separated from public life. Both matter, because each profoundly influences the other.

There are now thousands of citizen groups, all over the country, that are developing information and skills and relationships and programs to make democracy work on behalf of all. These groups consist of more than one hundred million Americans who volunteer an average of four hours a week to help causes or individuals. (Eight million of these are fourteen- to seventeen-year-olds.) Many have discovered that public life isn't just for officials. Their work diminishes apathy and despair, for it demonstrates that everyone is capable of helping to shape the direction of schools, the workplace, the community, and government.

As more and more citizens join in such endeavors, the prospects for a healthier political society in the twenty-first century can only expand.

William J. Clinton
1993–
(UPI/Corbis-Bettman)

Milton Meltzer has written nearly one hundred books for young readers and adults in the fields of history, biography, and social issues. Among his most recent titles are *Ten Queens: Portraits of Women of Power; Witchcraft and Witchhunts: A History of Persecution;* and *Driven From the Land: The Story of the Dust Bowl.*

TRUST AND OBEY:

A Personal Look at
Twentieth-Century Religion

My father was born on a farm in the valley of Virginia in 1893, or maybe 1894; the family records conflict, and there was no birth certificate. Nor was there electricity or central heat, much less a telephone, a radio, a television set, or a computer in the old farmhouse, part of which dated back to colonial times. But there was religion. There were family prayers every night, every member kneeling at his or her dining room chair and saying a prayer in turn. Scripture passages and the Westminster Catechisms, questions and answers about beliefs that Presbyterians had held to since 1647, were memorized and recited. My farmer grandfather was an elder, an ordained lay leader, and he took his wife and nine children to services at the Presbyterian Church every Sunday by horse and buggy.

In addition to his strong religious commitment, Grandfather Womeldorf, like most Presbyterians, believed in education and made sure his nine children had their share. The girls were sent away to nursing school or teacher training college. When my father's turn came, he walked (as his older brother had before him and his two younger brothers after him) the two miles into Lexington every day to attend Washington and Lee University. World War I was raging in Europe. When Dad was in his final year, the university formed an ambulance corps to be attached to the French army as the United States had not yet entered the war.

My father, who had never driven a car before and had been given exactly one brief practice drive in Pennsylvania, drove an ambulance across battlefields in France and Belgium until, less than two weeks before the Armistice, he was wounded so badly that, at one point, the French army doctor gave him up for dead. He returned to America minus his right leg, his lungs damaged by gas. No one thought he would live to be forty. He lived to be eighty-nine—or eighty-eight, depending on what year he was actually born.

In the years between his pronounced and actual deaths, he graduated from a Presbyterian seminary, married my mother, raised five children, and spent sixty years as a Presbyterian minister, eighteen of them as a missionary in China where the conditions of life were far more rugged than those of his childhood on a Virginia farm.

I was the middle of those five children, born in China in 1932. My father also believed in education. All five of us not only went to col-

Our family in 1936.
I'm between my parents.

lege, we took graduate degrees. My graduate degrees are in Bible and religious education. Following somewhat in my parents' footsteps, I spent four years as a missionary in Japan, and, since 1962, I have been married to a Presbyterian minister. So, between us, my father and I span the twentieth century. Although our outlooks differed somewhat, we both spent our lives closely related to the same mainline Protestant heritage, and it is from this however narrow vantage point that I have chosen to look at what happened during the twentieth century to religion in America.

When people speak of "Christian America," they are probably thinking of a time well before the Civil War when most influential Americans were white, Protestant, and of British descent. The nickname used for such people is "WASP" (and despite our German surname, my father and I are mostly WASP), meaning White, Anglo-Saxon Protestant.

That the time of WASP domination of religion and society should be regarded with wistfulness is peculiar, to say the least. The "Christian" nation that was America in the first two-thirds of the nineteenth century was a land where slavery was not only permitted, but protected. It was a place where prejudice and bias existed not only against persons of color, but against Jewish and Roman Catholic citizens as well, and any other religion was regarded as heathenism. It was a country that allowed the Irish fleeing from the potato famine to come in, work hard for very low wages, and then despised them for their poverty and Roman Catholic faith. It was a land where women of all backgrounds were given few opportunities and even fewer rights. None of my father's people owned slaves, and his mother's father was an outspoken opponent of slavery, but I cannot pretend that my family escaped many of the other prejudices of their time.

The Civil War dealt WASP America a terrible blow. A number of the large Protestant denominations divided into separate church bodies over the issues of slavery and states' rights. Perhaps Abraham Lincoln was one of the few persons of the time clear-eyed enough to see what was happening. In his second "Inaugural Address" (March 1865), he said:

> Both [North and South] read the same Bible, and pray to the same God; and each invokes His aid against the other. It may seem strange that any men should dare to ask a just God's assistance in wringing their bread from the sweat of other men's faces; but let us judge not that we be not judged. The prayers of

both could not be answered; that of neither has been answered fully. The Almighty has His own purposes.[1]

America, immersed in fratricidal bloodshed, hardly noticed a book published in England in 1859. But by the end of the century, this scientific treatise, Charles Darwin's *On the Origin of Species,* as well as his subsequent *Descent of Man* (1871), was the subject of hot debate on this side of the Atlantic. Both works were destined to profoundly change the way Americans thought about religion and its relation to scientific thought.

Darwin was not the first person to suggest that contemporary species may have evolved from lower forms of life, his own grandfather had said as much in 1803. But it was Charles Darwin's meticulous collecting of specimens from all around the world that provided the first real body of evidence for such a theory. In his *On the Origin of Species,* he put forth the proposition that species currently on earth had evolved over millions of years from other, more primitive species by a process of natural selection. Creatures who best adapted to a changing environment were more likely to survive—thus present-day species represented "the survival of the fittest."

Earlier, Sir Isaac Newton (1642–1727) proposed the idea of a material universe that ran itself without the need of divine intervention. This theory had seemed to make the God of the material world unnecessary. Now Darwin, in his theory that present forms of life had evolved from lower forms, seemed to eliminate the need for God as the creator of all living things. Even man, Darwin argued, was just the last step in an evolutionary chain—a process that would have taken millions of years.

Organized religion had lived in uneasy peace with scientific thought since the death of Galileo, who had advanced the un-Biblical notion that the earth revolved around the sun rather than vice versa. But the church had an even more serious problem with Darwin's theory. There was the question of when and the question of what.

At the end of the seventeenth century, Bishop James Ussher of the Church of England and a Hebrew scholar, John Lightfoot, had worked out what they believed to be the exact minute when the earth was created—9:00 A.M. on October 23rd, 4004 B.C. Following the account in the first chapter of Genesis, Ussher and Lightfoot maintained that all species on earth had been created in the first six days thereafter and had remained unchanged since. Beginning in 1701 and continuing well into the nineteenth century, this date for the Creation had been published in the King James Version of the Bible and was one of the beliefs of most churches at the time Darwin published his work. Now, however, geologists and paleontologists were insisting that the earth was millions of years old, and Darwin was claiming that everything in and on it had taken millennia to evolve. The plant and animal species whose specimens he had collected and classified didn't all date back to those first six days of 4004 B.C.

In America, the chief Protestant denominations, already torn in two by the issues of the Civil War, now became further divided. It would be too simple to say that they split along the lines of who believed Ussher versus who believed Darwin. But there were biblical scholars who began to apply scientific methods to the study of the Bible and others who felt that to do so would be to undermine the authority of the Bible.

In the face of astronomical discoveries, religious leaders had been forced to concede that Galileo had been right, that the earth was not the unmoving center of the universe. Now science was forcing another retreat. The geologic and paleontologic evidence of the immense age of the earth was pretty compelling, so there were attempts to modify the traditional view and still keep it in line with the Bible. One school of thought propounded what came to be known as the "Day-Age theory." Since a "day" was defined by the movement of the earth toward the sun, and since the sun was not created, according to the Genesis 1 account, until the fourth day, a day in this context would seem to indicate a long period of time that could be many years in duration, rather than a twenty-four-hour period.

Back in the 1940s, when I was young and took everything quite seriously, I remember a classmate asking me, "Do you believe in science or in God?" as though it would be impossible to believe in both. Imagining myself a pint-sized Christian soldier—after all, my father

Katherine in the seventh grade, 1943

was a Presbyterian minister— I opted, of course, for God, not realizing that I really didn't have to choose between them. But I was not alone. Many people throughout the twentieth century felt that a person had to line up on one side or the other. There are even those who mourn the death of "Christian America" and accuse "Science" of the murder.

I must confess that my father and I never had a lengthy conversation on the subject of science versus religion. But thinking back, I can't remember being told as a child that the world was created in 4004 B.C. And I know when I began thinking about the origins of creation, I was definitely a proponent of the Day-Age theory, though I wouldn't have known to call it that. I can remember quite well explaining to a friend that a "day" in Genesis couldn't mean twenty-four hours, because the sun wasn't even created until the fourth "day." And how did we measure our days? By the turning of earth toward and away from the sun. I suspect now that my father must have been a member of the Day-Age school, or it wouldn't have felt so comfortable and reasonable to me.

When I was young, it was very important to me for my father to think well of me. I think this is why, as I grew older and began more and more to look to science for answers about the natural world, I didn't want to talk to my father about it. I suspected we might not agree on such delicate subjects as the descent of humankind and literal interpretations of certain scriptural passages. Adam and Eve were not mythological personages to my father, nor was the devil. It is difficult to quibble about articles of belief with a man who lives his faith.

In the late nineteenth and early twentieth century, there was a great missionary movement in the mainline Protestant denominations. It swept college campuses, and many young men and women were caught up in it, promising to give their lives for service in those countries around the world where Christ was not yet known. The rallying cry of the movement was "The evangelization of the world in this generation!" The aim of these zealous young people was, in the words of one of its leaders, to give "to all men an adequate opportunity of knowing Jesus Christ as their Savior and becoming His real disciples."[2] It is probably no accident that this movement occurred at the same time that the United States and the chief nations of Europe were establishing colonies in lesser-developed countries. It was thought to be the "white man's burden" to bring enlightenment to the nonwhite world.

Both of my parents determined while still in college to become foreign missionaries. My mother always planned to go to China. I think my father had earlier thought of Africa but turned his sights on China while he was in seminary, maybe after he met my mother. I'm not sure about that. I do have, however, the letter he wrote his mother in 1922, when he told her not only that he was planning to go to China, but that he was planning to marry my mother. Reading between the lines, it sounds to me as though he'd never mentioned either China or Mary Goetchius to his family before. I don't think his family, as pious as they were, ever got over that double shock.

While my parents were falling in love, getting married, and sailing for China, Protestant America was becoming more and more divided theologically between those who felt their mission was to convert individuals who would then change their behavior and those who sought to reform society. Excerpts from two hymns show the contrast between these two emphases:

Fanny Crosby, whose hymns were sung in revival meetings as well as regular church services, wrote:

> *Rescue the perishing,*
> *Care for the dying,*
> *Snatch them in pity from sin and the grave;*
> *Weep o'er the erring one,*
> *Lift up the fallen,*
> *Tell them of Jesus the mighty to save.*

And Frank Mason North exemplified the gospel of the social reformers in these words:

My father with a Chinese friend, 1924

In haunts of wretchedness and
need,
On shadowed thresholds
fraught with fears,
From paths where hide the
lures of greed,
We catch the vision of Thy
tears.

My father was more at home with Fanny Crosby, and, as I grew older, I felt more at home with Frank Mason North; yet it was my father more than I who ministered in "haunts of wretchedness and need." But he was never a noble white man ministering to the benighted heathen. He had enormous respect for Chinese history and culture. His closest friend was the Chinese pastor with whom he worked. His Chinese was good enough so that he could joke with people in Chinese. They laughed with him and loved him.

In China, although his chief assignment was to run a boys' school and establish churches in the countryside, much of his time was spent in delivering food and medical help in time of famine and flood and war. (China has never lacked disasters.) The old gospel hymn I most associate with my father, and the one I always thought of as his favorite, is titled "Trust and Obey":

When we walk with the Lord
In the light of His Word
What a glory He sheds on our way!
While we do His good will,
He abides with us still,
And with all who will trust and obey.

Trust was the core of my father's faith. He felt he was walking with the Lord as friend with friend, sharing joys and sorrows, pain, disappointment, and even life's little triumphs. I think I can best illustrate this faith of my father's by sharing the first prayer he taught me. Most children of my generation said the bedtime prayer:

Now I lay me down to sleep,
I pray the Lord my soul to keep,
If I should die before I wake,
I pray the Lord my soul to take.

The prayer we learned was quite different in tone:

Precious Jesus,
Keep me through the night,
Safe from harm and danger
Till the morning light.

Both prayers date from a time when many children did not live to be adults, but our family prayer was one of trust rather than fear. Jesus was our friend, not someone who might snatch our lives away in the middle of the night.

Faith for my father was not adherence to a code of beliefs or a code of morality. My father was perhaps the most moral man I've ever known, but obedience for him was not confined to the "Thou shalt nots" of the Ten Commandments. To my father, obeying the Lord meant walking in the way Jesus walked, feeding the hungry, tending the sick, comforting the brokenhearted, defending the weak, and, yes, telling of the loving God who sent his Son to save a sick and sinful world.

Living and working in China, my father never got caught up in the battles over belief that divided Presbyterians and other denominations in America. My father wasn't given to arguments—certainly not to theological arguments. Although he himself was a conservative Christian, he felt that people could think differently and still respect and care for one another. When the priest at the Taoist temple in

Hwaian asked for a picture of Jesus to put in his display of gods (which included an ancient picture of Marco Polo), my father thought about it and decided to donate one they used in Sunday School. It didn't seem to him that Jesus would mind. When the local Roman Catholic missionary fell ill with suspected cholera, my father went immediately to his aid. The priest always credited my father with saving his life, though Dad was more skeptical. "If he'd really had cholera," Dad said, "I doubt if those old pills of mine would have done much good."

Even if he'd stayed in America, I don't believe my father would have spent time caught up in theological controversy. His understanding of faith was doing rather than talking. Whether he was taking food and clothing to flood victims or smuggling drugs through battle lines to the hospital upriver, he believed he was acting in obedience to the One in whom he trusted.

A moral reform movement that began in the nineteenth century and continued into the twentieth, uniting many WASPs, both liberal and conservative, was the temperance or prohibition movement. This culminated in 1919 with the ratification of the Eighteenth Amendment to the Constitution, which prohibited "the manufacture, sale, or transportation of intoxicating liquors." Prohibition as national policy failed miserably, but my parents were certainly, though not noisily, teetotalers and would have supported Prohibition.

None of their children followed them in this, but we all assumed that neither of them had ever, or would ever, taste alcohol. Then one day my brother thought to ask Dad about his stint with the French army in World War I. When he was in France, had he ever drunk any wine? My father snorted. "You don't think I would have been dumb enough to drink *water*, do you? It would have killed me."

My father was not a political animal, but he was a great admirer of William Jennings Bryan, who ran for president in 1896, 1900, and 1908. I was not comfortable with his choice of hero. When I thought of Bryan, I saw him as portrayed in the play *Inherit the Wind:* a tired old man trying to hold back the flood tide of history. The play is about the Scopes trial in Tennessee. In 1925, the state of Tennessee passed a law forbidding the teaching of Darwin's theory of evolution in the public schools. When high school biology teacher John Scopes defied the law, a trial resulted that was as famous in its time as the O. J. Simpson murder trial is in ours.

Clarence Darrow, a famous criminal lawyer, led the team defending Scopes, and William Jennings Bryan offered to aid the prosecution with his famous oratory. "The evolutionary hypothesis, carried to its logical conclusion," he said, "disputes every vital truth of the Bible." Bryan concluded that "this case is no longer local. . . . [It] has assumed the proportions of a battle-royal between unbelief that attempts to speak through so-called science and the defenders of the Christian faith, speaking through the legislators of Tennessee."[3]

Technically, Bryan's team won. The jury convicted Scopes and fined him $100. The play makes Darrow the hero of the trial and does not treat the ailing Bryan very kindly. In fact, Bryan died almost immediately after the completion of the trial and achieved something of a martyrlike status among those devoted to his anti-Darwinian cause.

I always supposed my father liked Bryan because he was a conservative Presbyterian and a defender of the biblical account of Creation. But Bryan was more than that. He was a staunch proponent of the rights of farmers and workers in the face of the greed and lust for power of the financiers and industrialists of his time. He was far ahead of his contemporaries as he worked for fairness for women. He even believed women should be allowed to vote. As secretary of state under Woodrow Wilson, he resigned when he felt Wilson, against his campaign pledge, was pushing the nation unnecessarily into World War I.

When I learned more about my father's political hero, it seemed sad to me that Bryan is best remembered for attacking the teaching of evolution in the public schools. He was a great man, even if I do disagree with his convictions about evolution.

By the end of 1940, much of the world was already at war. The American embassy in China ordered American families to leave the country as soon as possible. China, all during the years my parents lived and worked there, was a land of war and civil unrest. My family was forced to flee our home so often that my mother referred to us jokingly as the "China fleas." We had just been "fleas" in 1938 and spent a year in the States; but now, once again we would have to leave.

The America to which my parents brought us in December 1940 was quite different from the one they had left in 1923. It was a nation where the influence of WASP society had shrunk dramatically. The country was still reeling from the Great Depression. The optimism of the early twenties had long since disappeared. The mass immigrations of the late nineteenth and early twentieth centuries had brought thousands of penniless Eastern European Jews and Italian and Irish Roman Catholics to our shores. Now the children of those immigrants had grown up, become educated and established. Some of them, indeed, had become wealthy and powerful.

In addition, more fundamentalist factions of the larger Protestant denominations had split off to become new denominations and then, as in the case of the Presbyterians, resplit when fresh arguments arose. Entirely new sects were formed, a number with a Pentecostal emphasis on speaking in tongues. These Christians believed that the Holy Spirit came to them as it had in New Testament times, causing them to praise God in an unknown language. The Pentecostal movement (named after the biblical Feast of Pentecost, during which the early disciples received the gift of tongues) has since grown stronger and claimed adherents in the mainline denominations, as well as in the newer sects and denominations.

The rise of Adolf Hitler in the 1930s caused many European Jews to seek refuge abroad. To its shame, "Christian America" was not welcoming. Some Jews did manage to come in. One, a German physicist named Albert Einstein, was already on his way to achieving the rank of a Galileo or a Newton as a brilliant theorist. Einstein would indeed revolutionize scientific thought about the universe and, interestingly enough, bring about a renewed scientific interest in religion.

The horrors of World War II, especially the Holocaust and the nuclear destruction of Hiroshima and Nagasaki, have made many thinking people question the existence and/or nature of God. This anguished agnosticism persists and cannot be easily dismissed by religious people.

There was, to be sure, a brief resurgence in the 1950s of the mainline WASP churches, but it proved to be a postwar boom that has since deflated.

The Roman Catholic Church under Pope John XXIII had a burst of modernization and renewal during the 1960s, when the Pope reached out in an attempt to unite Christiandom once more. But with John's death, later popes have emphasized more traditional thinking, and the more overt attempts at unity have ceased. However, the legacy of John XXIII is still felt in American Christianity, where there is, in many places, a desire by both Protestants and Roman Catholics to work closely together and learn from each other.

The churchgoing fifties gave way to the unrest of the late sixties and early seventies. African-American churches, which have consistently served as the vital center of their communities, took the lead in a long overdue movement to secure for black Americans the full rights of citizenship. On the list of great Americans of the twentieth century, the name of an African-American Baptist minister will invariably appear. Martin Luther King, Jr., inspired by the Bible and the teachings of Mahatma Gandhi, led a nonviolent movement for the human and civil rights of black America.

WASP America was divided in its response to the movement. Indeed, white Christians were often among its harshest critics and persecutors. But there were individual white Americans, Jewish, Christian, and nonreligious—who joined the marches led by King and his African-American Southern Christian Leadership Conference. In the words of the movement's most famous song:

Black and white together
We shall overcome.

I heard Dr. King speak in 1955 before he was really famous, and I was profoundly impressed. During the early years of the movement, I was in Japan and could watch the marches and sit-ins only from afar. Later, I stayed home with the children while my husband went to Alabama to march and go to jail with his fellow marchers. I was very proud of him. When Dr. King was assassinated during Easter week

1968, the shock was felt all over America. I felt, as many Americans must have, both a profound personal grief and a conviction that my country had been irreparably wounded.

Dr. King, a winner of the Nobel Peace Prize, had been severely criticized for opposing the war in Vietnam. For him, opposition to the war was in line with his opposition to racism and his devotion to non-violence, but for many Americans, this opposition seemed anti-patriotic. Initially, most American churches backed the war, though the eloquence of King and other leaders and the protests of American students eventually turned much of the public against the conflict. Despite the fact that there were religious leaders involved in the anti-war movement, the students did not look to the churches for moral leadership in their struggle.

Billy Graham visits my parents in Winchester, Virginia, 1976.

During the late 1960s, WASP culture suffered a loss of authority in society, and the traditional WASP churches saw declining memberships. Conservative Christians like my father, however, had a powerful new spokesperson. The Reverend Billy Graham, who came out of the Southern Baptist Church, began preaching to larger and larger crowds. Dr. Graham, unlike many charismatic preachers, did not seek to form his own church. Instead, his crusades worked closely with local churches, and persons who became Christians through his preaching were urged to join already existing congregations. No one had seen evangelistic campaigns of this magnitude since the days of Dwight L. Moody in the late nineteenth century and Billy Sunday in the first decades of the twentieth. Dr. Graham preached to millions around the world, calling them to turn away from sin and believe in Jesus Christ, who would transform their lives in this world and take them to heaven after death.

Although my father admired Martin Luther King Jr., he felt much more comfortable with Billy Graham. He felt especially drawn to Dr. Graham not only by the power and effectiveness of his preaching, but because of Mrs. Graham. Ruth Bell Graham had been born in China, ten miles away from our home in Hwaian. Her father was the missionary doctor we all went to, who delivered both me and my younger sister. It was for Dr. Bell's hospital that my father smuggled drugs.

Billy Graham has continued for nearly half a century to be the greatest single voice for conservative Christians. He has been the advisor and confidant of American presidents and no history of American twentieth-century religious life would be complete without his name.

In sheer numbers, growth in religion in the last decade of the century seems more tied to a charismatic leader than to a system of belief, though the belief espoused by the leader is usually fundamentalist or markedly conservative. I say, "religion," rather than "Christianity," because it seems to me there is a fundamentalist resurgence in Judaism and Islam, as well as in Christianity. My father has been dead for fifteen years, so I can only guess what his analysis of the contemporary religious scene would be. But I think he would be saddened by the arrogance of some leaders of the religious right. As conservative as he was, he sought always to unify rather than to divide, and he was too humble to assume that his own beliefs were infallible.

One of the most dramatic developments in WASP churches that has occurred in the last one hundred years is the place of women. Our own Presbyterian Church, which was the southern group that came out of the slavery states' rights dispute, was slower than most mainline Protestant groups in giving women the right to hold office and to become ordained clergy. The Roman Catholic Church and many of the more conservative and fundamentalist churches still do not ordain women, but in most Protestant denominations, women not only serve as pastors, but have been elected bishops or to other high offices.

This was one area in which my father differed early on from most of his conservative colleagues. He voted for the ordination of women. Those who thought they could count on him to cast a conservative vote on most issues were surprised and, I imagine, a bit annoyed.

When questioned, he answered that he believed his vote was in line with what the Bible taught, citing the words of the apostle Paul: "There is neither Jew or Greek, there is neither bond nor free, there is neither male nor female; for you are all one in Christ Jesus."

The women's movement within the church has profoundly changed the language in which prayers are said and hymns are sung. The change to inclusive language makes many people uncomfortable. After nearly two thousand years of speaking of God as Father, Son, and Holy Spirit, it is hard, especially for older people, to shift to language like Creator, Redeemer, and Spirit. Although the Bible itself has always used both male and female images for God, the church has so long emphasized the male images that it comes as a shock to many to think of God not only as Father, but also as Mother.

Even though my denomination would not, when I was young, allow me to go to seminary and become a minister, I decided to become a missionary. I studied in the graduate school that my church had founded to train lay workers and then applied to work in Japan. Before the mission board would approve me, they required that the leaders of my local congregation examine my beliefs. I reread all the creeds and catechisms in the Book of Confessions and found myself troubled. The Puritan churchmen who gathered at Westminster Abbey in 1647 laid the foundations of the Presbyterian Church in the Westminster Confession and Catechisms. But how was I, three hundred years later, to promise that I believed such statements as "the wicked who know not God, and obey not the gospel of Jesus Christ, shall be cast into eternal torments."

"I can't say that," I said to my father, who was also my pastor. I was thinking of the shepherd in Jesus' story who never gave up searching until the lost sheep was found. "I don't think God ever gives up loving, ever." I may have raised my voice when I said this.

At any rate, my father smiled, reached over, and patted my knee. "It's all right," he said. "You don't have to adhere to every line of the confessions. You'll only be asked to accept the 'essential tenets of the Reformed faith.'"

"Oh, well," I said with relief. "I can do that."

But of course one of the most essential of those tenets is the Bible's great commandment: "You shall love the Lord your God with all your heart, and with all your soul, and with all your strength, and with all your mind; and your neighbor as yourself."

The Presbyterians got that from Jesus, and Jesus got it from the Hebrew Bible. We can only guess at the age of the great commandment, and we're still stumbling over it, Jew and Christian alike.

As one of those stumbling Christians, I have found help in loving God with my mind in a surprising place. In the last few years, I have read more books written by scientists than books written by theologians. Perhaps this is because, like my father, I seek for unity rather than strife. I think I have Einstein to thank for this change. He spent the last years of his life pursuing a unity between the immensity of the universe and the minuteness of subatomic particles. "I want," he said once, "to know how God created this world. I am not interested in this or that phenomenon. I want to know His thoughts, the rest are details."

The writings of today's scientific thinkers cause me to marvel at the universe, so that I am filled with wonder. It thrills me to read a physicist arguing for the existence of God, as Edmund Whittaker does. "There is no ground for supposing," he says, "that matter and energy existed before [the Big Bang] and were suddenly galvanized into action. For what could distinguish that moment from all other moments in eternity? It is simple to postulate creation *ex nihilo*— Divine will constituting Nature from nothingness."[4]

My father and I in 1980

And then I remember something that happened toward the end of my father's life.

He showed me an article he had been reading about a man who had mounted a trip to the mountain thought to be Mt.

Ararat, which in Genesis is where Noah landed the ark after the flood. The man claimed that he had found the remains of the ark, thereby proving the truth of the biblical account. "What do you think of that?" Dad asked me, and it was apparent that he really wanted my opinion.

"Well, I very much doubt that what he found was really the remains of Noah's ark," I said. Being trained by Newton and René Descartes to question everything, it seemed unlikely that the remains of a wooden boat would last thousands of years or that anyone could prove from the remains that it had been sailed by Noah. "But even if he had found the ark, it really wouldn't affect my faith one way or the other." What I meant, but didn't say to my father, was that many early civilizations have a flood story, and my trust in the God of the Bible doesn't depend on the accuracy of the details of the stories in Genesis.

My father didn't comment on what I said, and we never discussed the matter again. He did look a little disappointed, though. I think he really would have liked scientific corroboration for the biblical account of the flood, and for me to indicate that it didn't matter bothered him.

But are my father and I so different? I look to modern physics for a confirmation of the existence and work of God—something that science is incapable of providing. There is no proof for religious belief, whatever our wistful longings for objective proof might be, and, in fact, neither my father nor I have based our faith on scientific proofs.

The great Protestant theologian of this century, Karl Barth, was once asked to say in one sentence the essence of his faith. Barth replied in the words of a nineteenth century children's hymn:

Jesus loves me,
This I know,
For the Bible
Tells me so.

My belief about God is like Barth's. It comes from the Bible story of

God's love for the world. St. Paul tells us that Jesus is the image of the unseen God. Thus the God I have learned about through Jesus is a God of unfailing goodness and love.

Years ago I was teaching a fifth-grade Sunday School class the story of the Prodigal Son. In this story, Jesus, trying to explain what God is like, tells about a loving father who not only forgives his wayward son, but throws a big party upon his return. The older brother who stayed home and behaved himself is furious. But the father goes out to his older son and begs him to forget his petulant self-righteousness and join in his joy that the lost son and brother has returned. I waited to see if any of those ten-year-olds could understand the story I'd just told. "I can," said a boy, "my dad is just like that."

So is mine, I thought.

I realize that I have been very blessed. I had a father who didn't always agree with what I thought, who didn't always approve of what I did, but who truly loved and respected me. I know that, because of him, it is much easier for me to believe in a God who not only made the world, but who loves all the creatures in it. I learned about this God from my father.

I also learned that learning about and trusting in are two different things. Nothing that I believe about God can be proved, and because I am human and faulty, my beliefs about God will always be inadequate, and I must continue to be open to what other people in their different understanding about God can teach me.

But faith is much more than belief. It is a journey of trust. My father taught me, by word and by example, that we move on through the years trusting the God that Jesus revealed to us, seeing as Jesus did that the whole world is loved by God. And when we love our neighbors, we slowly learn to know and love more fully God, who is invisible and otherwise unknowable. This is the faith I seek to carry with me into the uncertainties of the next century.

As my father would say, "Trust and obey."

Katherine Paterson is the author of more than twenty-five books, including thirteen novels, for young people. Two of these novels are National Book Award winners: *The Master Puppeteer* and *The Great Gilly Hopkins,* which was also the single Honor Book for the 1979 Newbery Medal. She received the Newbery Medal for *Bridge to Terabithia* and for *Jacob Have I Loved.* Her books have been published in twenty-two languages, and she is the 1998 recipient of the most distinguished international award in children's literature, the Hans Christian Andersen Medal. Ms. Paterson was born in China and came to the United States at the start of World War II. She and her husband, Reverend John B. Paterson, have four children and four grandchildren.

Notes

1. Lincoln's quote is cited in Mark A. Noll, *A History of Christianity in the United States and Canada.* (Grand Rapids: Eerdman's, 1992), pp. 322–323.

2. Noll, *A History of Christianity*, p. 291.

3. Janelle Rohr, Editor. *Science and Religion: Opposing Viewpoints* (St. Paul, MN: Greenhaven Press, 1988), pp. 49, 50.

4. Quoted in Robert M. Augros and George N. Stancin, *The New Story of Science* (New York: Bantam Books, 1986), p. 63.

LAURENCE PRINGLE

HEROES FOR THE WHOLE EARTH

Imagine this: In the early 1900s, you finish making a time-travel machine in your family's barn. You get in, shut the door, turn the crank handle to start the machine—and you suddenly leap ahead one hundred years. You open the door to find yourself in the early twenty-first century.

You are still in North America, but, oh, how things have changed! For starters, there are the automobiles and trucks. A century ago, they numbered in the thousands. Now cars and highways and parking lots seem to be everywhere. And you don't have to turn a crank to start a car. They start by using electricity. Just that word—"electricity"— brings to mind an amazing variety of things new to you: neon lights, radio, television, computers, video games.

You are full of questions. What is this stuff called "plastic"? And how can humans fly through the air in machines? Everywhere you go, there are mind-boggling sights and sounds—the clothes, the music. Some of the amazing sights are at the beach. Who could have predicted a century ago that girls and women would shed those long-skirted swimming costumes?

After a few days, you begin to get used to some of the extraordinary changes, but you continue to notice others. For example, many people wear colorful T-shirts with words and pictures on them. Some are of sports teams or musical groups whose names are new to you.

Other T-shirts have messages. One shows an appealing picture of a wolf and the words SAVE THE WOLVES. Another shows flying bats and the words GENTLE ALLIES, ESSENTIAL FRIENDS.

This is puzzling. Why would anyone want to protect wolves and bats? You thought they were harmful, "bad" animals, but you ask anyway, and people tell you about the value of these animals in nature. They use ideas and words that are new to you: ecology, endangered species, environment. And every day, you see more signs that people are concerned about the environment.

Until the 1950s, power companies used to urge people to use more, *more,* MORE! Now advertisements tell people how to use less electricity and natural gas. You see vast amounts of glass, plastic, and paper being collected for recycling. You learn how buildings, cars, and appliances are constructed to save energy and reduce pollution. The smoky, soot-filled city skies of a century ago are much clearer now. And, despite a landscape that has been vastly changed by people, many wild places have been spared. Even swamps are valued as homes for wildlife and as natural flood controls and protectors of water supplies. In your time, the early 1900s, swamps were thought to be useless—something to be filled in or drained.

It seems that many of the ideas of the early 1900s about wildlife and other natural resources have changed—and they have. The past century turned out to be a century of conservation. The conservation movement, which began to be called the "environmental movement," caused dramatic changes in the way people think about nature.

The roots of this great social and political movement go further back than 1900. The term "conservation" was coined in 1864; land for Yellowstone National Park was protected in 1872; millions of woodland acres that would later be national forests were saved in the 1890s. However, most people of the early twentieth century still thought of nature as something to conquer and use without consequences. They dumped wastes freely into rivers and lakes. Whole forests were felled without replanting. Most wildlife could be killed year-round. And wild predators—hawks, wolves, mountain lions—were favorite targets because they were considered useless "vermin."

Today, more and more people think of themselves as nature's partners, not nature's masters. There are many laws aimed at protecting wild habitats and reducing pollution. None of this great change was accomplished easily. It took the work of many people: hunters, fishers, bird-watchers, writers, philosophers, scientists. When the federal goverment or a state took steps to protect nature, it was often a result of the efforts of one person or a small group. Now, looking back over the last century, these people can be called "conservation heroes."

Only a few of these heroes were elected officials. One was the man who became president of the United States in 1901: Theodore "Teddy" Roosevelt. TR, as he was called, loved the outdoors. He hunted, fished, hiked. With firsthand knowledge, he saw the need to halt the loss of forests, wildlife, and other resources. He sought advice from Gifford Pinchot, a professional forester, and John Muir, a writer and outdoorsman who urged the protection of wilderness areas.

TR became "the conservation president." His leadership and crafty use of laws led to fifty-one areas around the nation protected as wildlife refuges and other, larger areas saved to eventually become national parks. This upset the timber and mining companies that wanted to exploit resources everywhere. They influenced some of the presidents that followed TR, who tried to undo his accomplishments. They did not succeed, however, because Teddy Roosevelt had helped make conservation a national concern.

Still, some early attempts to take better care of natural resources failed because so little was known about the workings of nature. For example, men worked hard to prevent and put out every forest fire. Eventually, scientists learned that forests and their wildlife actually benefit from an occasional fire. The heat from a fire releases the seeds from the cones of some pine trees. Minerals in a fire's ashes help new plant growth to flourish. Grazing and seed-eating animals find a new wealth of food. By the 1980s, some fires were being allowed to burn in western national parks and national forests. Other fires were even set—and closely monitored—by park rangers.

Several old notions about wildlife were also discarded. A forester named Aldo Leopold learned from his experience of trying to manage woodlands and wildlife, then shared his wisdom in an extraordinary book called *A Sand County Almanac*. Leopold worked in New Mexico.

In 1920, he spoke with approval of the goal of killing the last wolf or mountain lion in that state. He believed, as everyone then did, that killing predators would lead to thriving herds of deer. But Leopold was open to new ideas and evidence. By 1938, he was teaching a course at the University of Wisconsin on wildlife ecology.

Aldo Leopold offered a scientist's wisdom about how humans are part of nature, not nature's masters. (Aldo Leopold Foundation, Archives)

Until about 1970, "ecology" was a mystery word to the average U.S. citizen, and yet Leopold was teaching and writing about it before midcentury. Ecology is the study of the relationship between living things and their surroundings. One thing Leopold learned about ecology is that wolves and other predators are vital members of plant and animal communities. Usually, predators cannot catch the most healthy prey; they tend to kill animals that are diseased, injured, or otherwise not fit. By removing them, wolves and other predators actually benefit the deer and other animal populations upon which they prey.

Leopold regretted having promoted their death. After his own death, public attitudes toward predators began to change. In the 1990s he would have been delighted to see wolves released to live again in Yellowstone National Park and other wild areas.

In *A Sand County Almanac,* published in 1949, Aldo Leopold wrote about ecology and the relationship of humans to nature. His book is one of the most important written in the twentieth century because it showed that there are sound scientific reasons to protect wildlife and natural areas. With the support of ecologists and other scientists, the conservation movement gained strength.

Time and again, the conservation movement also gained momentum because one person took action and fought for change. At Hawk Mountain in eastern Pennsylvania it was a woman, Rosalie Edge. Until 1932, Hawk Mountain was a favorite spot for hunters to shoot hundreds of hawks. They mistakenly believed they were doing good by killing predators. Rosalie Edge saw photographs of the hawk slaughter. She helped raise money to buy the land, establishing the world's first sanctuary for birds of prey. Since 1934, Hawk Mountain has become a world-renowned place to watch and count hawks and eagles as they migrate south.

In 1962, another woman became an environmental hero on a much larger scale. She wrote a book that led to changes in people's views all over the world. The book was *Silent Spring;* the author, Rachel Carson.

When Rachel Carson was a college student, she felt she had to choose between being a scientist and being a writer. A professor told her she could be both, and she eventually was, working as an aquatic biologist and gradually becoming a gifted writer.

Her writing success allowed her to stop work with the Fish and Wildlife Service, but she continued to keep informed about the findings of wildlife biologists. Her research led to *Silent Spring,* a book warning about the possible harm of long-lasting insecticides to all sorts of wildlife—and even to humans. For the first time, many people became aware that they occupied the last site on the food chain, and that little was known about the long-term effects of certain chemicals in their food.

Rachel Carson warned that people, as well as wildlife, can be harmed by changes in the environment. (UPI/Corbis-Bettman)

Silent Spring was about threats to birds and fish, but also to people. It was about protecting wildlife, but also about protecting humans. It was a step in the change of the conservation movement to the environmental movement. Another big step was the first Earth Day, on April 22, 1970. Millions of people, many of them students, gathered at huge rallies and street fairs to express their concern about the environment.

That first Earth Day was a wake-up call for many politicians. It led to a flurry of new laws aimed at reducing pollution and giving better protection to the land and its life, including endangered species. In the wake of this legislation, people had high hopes for a healthier environment. Today, many do breathe cleaner air and swim in cleaner water, but environmental problems proved to be much more difficult than anyone had imagined. And the fast-growing human population needed more food, burned more fuels, and created new problems.

By the 1980s, tropical forests were being burned or cleared of trees at the rate of six acres a minute. Whole habitats that were homes to unknown species of plants and animals were being destroyed. The numbers of fish in the oceans were being rapidly depleted. Even the earth's atmosphere was being changed in ways that could cause great harm to life on earth.

Fortunately there were—and are—more heroes trying to solve these and other problems. Some are scientists, some are leaders of environmental groups, and some are ordinary citizens, young and old.

Two of these scientists, Sherwood Rowland and Mario Molina, were researchers at the University of California at Irvine. In 1974 they discovered that certain chemicals entering the earth's atmosphere could harm the ozone layer which protects living things from most ultraviolet (UV) light. UV light is powerful enough to cause skin cancer and also damage crops and the tiny organisms that are the foundation of many food chains. In addition to publishing their findings in science journals, Rowland and Molina felt they had a responsibility to inform the public. They became targets for criticism from industries that would be affected if their ozone-depletion theory was correct.

The discoveries of Mario Molina and Sherwood Rowland led to further discoveries about chemicals that harm the Earth's protective ozone layer.
(UPI/Corbis-Bettman)

Gradually, other researchers around the world found evidence to confirm Rowland and Molina's ideas. This led to an international agreement in 1987 to ban production of the chemicals that destroy ozone, especially compounds called "CFCs" (chlorofluorocarbons) that were used as coolants in refrigerators and air conditioners. In 1995, Rowland, Molina, and another ozone researcher were awarded the Nobel Prize in chemistry for discovering the chemical threat to the earth's ozone layer.

The experience of Sherwood Rowland and Mario Molina was all too common in the last quarter of the twentieth century. Scientists who made key discoveries of threats to the environment were sometimes threatened themselves. They were sometimes called "un-American" because their findings could lead to changes in industries, including a possible loss of jobs. However, the scientists were simply reporting the truth about the environment in which everyone lives.

One scientist who was an expert on mammals was considered odd because he advocated the protection of bats. In 1982, he founded an organization called Bat Conservation International. Merlin Tuttle said, "Imagine what it's like to start an organization whose sole purpose is conservation of one of the least popular groups of animals on earth."

However, as people learned the truth about bats, Bat Conservation International grew in membership and in influence. By 1999, the organization had more than fourteen thousand members worldwide. It had helped protect numerous bat colonies in North America. In the long run, perhaps its most important work was teaching people in many countries about the value of bats—as predators of insects and, in the tropics, as pollinators of flowers and dispersers of the seeds of many trees.

As the twenty-first century dawned, scientists of many kinds supported the environmental movement. They included atmospheric scientists who found evidence that humans are causing the whole global climate to grow warmer. They even included economists who saw the folly of continuing to ignore harm to the environment when the costs of a new project or product were assessed. As one noneconomist put it, "In the long term, the environment and the economy are the same thing—if it's unenvironmental, it's uneconomic." This wisdom came from Mollie Beattie, the first woman to be named director of the U. S. Fish and Wildlife Service.

One of the most influential modern-day scientists is Edward O. Wilson. He is a world-renowned authority on ants, yet he is much more. Like Rachel Carson, he writes gracefully about science. His books have won awards, stirred debate, and sparked research. His

Renowned biologist Edward O. Wilson said, "Environmentalists have been looked on as the dreamers of the world, when in fact they are the realists." (UPI/Corbis-Bettman)

stature as a highly respected scientist has added more credibility to the environmental movement. Wilson is one of the world's great champions of saving biodiversity—the extraordinary but dwindling variety of life on earth.

For every environmental hero who has been world famous, there are thousands who have been known only in a local area or whose efforts on a local issue have led to national recognition. One such figure is Lois Gibbs. In 1978, she was a young housewife in western New York who became concerned about the health of her sons, who attended school near a landfill containing toxic wastes—twenty thousand tons of buried chemicals. The area was called Love Canal.

Gibbs led efforts to get state and federal authorities to deal with the toxic wastes and protect residents. Hundreds of families were relocated. Gibbs founded a national group that is now called the Center for Health, Environment, and Justice. It aims to help local community groups get toxic waste sites cleaned up and fight construction of hazardous projects.

The organization Lois Gibbs founded is just one of several thousand conservation and environmental groups in the United States. Only a few of these groups existed before 1900. Now there are several dozen well-known national groups. Some of them, such as the Sierra Club, the Nature Conservancy, and the National Audubon Society, have local chapters in many communities. In addition, there are countless smaller "grass-roots" organizations. An estimated twenty-five million people belong to one or more environmental groups.

The staffs of numerous environmental organizations include lawyers, scientists, and other professionals who could earn bigger salaries if they worked elsewhere. They choose to earn less because they believe that working on environmental issues is so important. And some of them first became active when they were students.

In 1973, Andy Lipkis was fifteen years old and lived near Los Angeles. He had enjoyed attending camp in forests east of the city and was alarmed to learn that smog drifting through the air from Los Angeles was killing many trees in those forests. That summer, he and other campers worked hard for three weeks planting an area with young trees that could survive in polluted air. He launched a new environmental group, TreePeople, and did not know he had begun his life's work.

By the end of the century, TreePeople was responsible for planting nearly two million trees. Many were planted in city and suburban areas, to help reduce pollution, to offer cooling shade, and to provide habitat for wildlife. Some were planted overseas. Fruit trees, for example, were sent to Africa to provide sources of food.

Lois Gibbs' career as an environmental leader began because she was a mother who tried to protect her own children and others from the effects of a toxic waste dump. (UPI/Corbis-Bettman)

Planting native trees and shrubs is just one action that many thousands of young people have taken to help the environment. From elementary schools to college campuses, young people decided that they did not have to wait until adulthood to act. "Just start with doing something small. Small things add up," is the advice of Melissa Poe, who was nine years old when she founded Kids for a Clean Environment (Kids FACE) in 1989. By the turn of the century, this organization had more than three hundred thousand members in thousands of chapters worldwide.

Other student groups include Kids Against Pollution, Children for a Safe Environment, and Children's Rain Forest U. S. There are many more. Often, most of the actions these groups take are not controversial. They promote recycling in their own schools and communities. They may clean beaches of litter or "adopt" a local stream or other wild habitat. They might raise money to help save a tropical rain forest from destruction.

Inevitably, however, many young environmentalists take political action. They write letters or ask people to sign petitions in order to influence decisions—locally, in state capitals, or nationally in Washington,

Learning about nature is a step toward caring about it, and millions of young people now care enough to take action to help the environment.
(Michael Dolittle)

D.C. Sometimes politicians and others dismiss such "kid" efforts. However, young people who show that they have a good understanding of an issue can earn respect, and get results.

In Coral Springs, Florida, teacher Charles deVeney and his class of teenagers were concerned about the steady loss of wild places in their community. In 1987, they tried to preserve a sixty-eight-acre woodland near their school. The city planned to make a park, but one with many soccer fields. Thousands of trees would be felled. The natural forest would be gone.

The students formed an organization called Save What's Left. They wrote letters to the city commissioners, suggesting other sites for soccer fields—to no avail. They took a more drastic step, holding signs alongside a road and seeking signatures of passing residents on a petition. In a few days, they had more than thirty-five hundred signatures.

This caught the attention of the city commissioners and of other people who eventually became involved. After two more years of political action a county bond issue was approved by voters. The money it provided saved the forest as well as thirteen other natural sites in the county.

At the beginning of the new century, students of Coral Springs High School continued to help Save What's Left in their community. Like other young people who were involved in environmental actions, they knew that the twenty-first century would bring new problems, new challenges. But they knew from experience that people—young and old—working together have the power to change things, to help take better care of the environment.

The past one hundred years have been called the "conservation century." The conservation movement began with concern about saving wildlife and wilderness, then grew, changed, and evolved into the environmental movement. It has influenced the attitudes and actions of people all over the world. But much more needs to be done. If it isn't, humans may wipe out most of the diversity of life on earth and make devastating changes in the earth's climate.

Perhaps the next one hundred years will be called the "environment century." If so, we can thank the pioneers of the past. Some were famous, many were little known. They were males and females, kids and adults. They were all heroes for the whole earth.

Laurence Pringle studied wildlife conservation at Cornell University and the University of Massachusetts and was a science teacher and a magazine editor before becoming a full-time freelance writer in 1970. His eighty-fourth book, *One Room School,* was published in 1998. Mr. Pringle's books about nature, ecology, and environmental problems have won praise and awards, including the 1998 Orbis Pictus Award for Outstanding Nonfiction for Children from the National Council of Teachers of English, for *An Extraordinary Life: The Story of a Monarch Butterfly.*

FOR FURTHER READING

Looking Back at Looking Forward
by Russell Freedman

Verne, Jules. *From the Earth to the Moon,* trans. Lowell Blair. New York: Bantam, 1993.

Verne, Jules. *2000 Leagues Under the Sea*. New York: Bantam, 1985.

Wells, H. G. *The Time Machine*. New York: Tor Books, 1995.

Wells, H. G. *The First Men in the Moon,* ed. David Lake. New York: Oxford University Press, 1996.

Wells, H. G. *The War of the Worlds*. New York: New American Library, 1996.

Immigrants All
by Eve Bunting

Ashabranner, Brent. *Still a Nation of Immigrants*. New York: Dutton, 1993.

Blumenthal, Shirley, and Jerome S. Ozer. *Coming to America: Immigrants from the British Isles*. New York: Delacorte, 1980.

Bouvier, Leon F. *Think About Immigration: Social Diversity in the U.S.* New York: Walker & Co., 1988.

Fermi, Laura. *Illustrious Immigrants*. Chicago: University of Chicago Press, 1968.

Garver, Susan, and Paula McGuire. *Coming to North America: From Mexico, Cuba, and Puerto Rico*. New York: Delacorte, 1981.

Greenleaf, Barbara Kaye. *America Fever*. New York: Four Winds Press, 1970.

Hartmann, Edward G. *American Immigration*. Minnesota: Lerner, 1979.

Heaps, Willard A. *The Story of Ellis Island*. New York: Seabury Press, 1967.

Los Angeles Times, July 4, 1998—"Racing to America," William C. Repel; reprinted by *New York Times*, July 19, 1998.

Siegel, Beatrice. *Sam Ellis's Island*. New York: Four Winds Press, 1985.

America's First World War
by Albert Marrin

Berry, Henry. *Make the Kaiser Dance*. Garden City, NY: Doubleday, 1978.

Churchill, Allen. *Over Here: An Informal Re-creation of the Home Front in World War I*. New York: Dodd, Mead, 1968.

Ellis, Edward Robb. *Echoes of Distant Thunder: Life in the United States, 1914–1918*. New York: Coward McCann Gohegan, 1975.

Harries, Meirion, and Susie Harries. *The Last Days of Innocence: America at War, 1917–1918*. New York: Random House, 1997.

Kennedy, David M. *Over Here: The First World War in American Society*. New York: Oxford University Press, 1980.

A Hundred Years of Wheels and Wings
by Jim Murphy

Clymer, Floyd. *Those Wonderful Old Automobiles*. New York: McGraw Hill, 1953.

Gerard, Patrick. *Flying Machines*. Milwaukee, Wisconsin: Raintree, 1980.

Giblin, James Cross. *Charles A. Lindbergh: A Human Hero*. New York: Clarion, 1997.

Jeffers, David. *Flight, Fliers, and Flying Machines*. New York: Franklin Watts, 1991.

Jensen, Oliver. *The American Heritage History of Railroads in America*. New York: American Heritage/Bonanza Books, 1981.

Smith, Mark, and Naomi Black. *America on Wheels: Tales and Trivia of the Automobile*. New York: Morrow, 1986.

Stein, Ralph. *The Treasury of the Automobile*. New York: Golden Press, 1961.

Vecsey, George, and George C. Dade. *Getting Off the Ground: The Pioneers of Aviation Speak for Themselves*. New York: Dutton, 1979.

The Century Babies Became Pros
by Bruce Brooks

Bradley, Bill. *Life on the Run*. New York: Vintage, 1995.

Dryden, Ken. *The Game*. New York: Penguin Sports Library, 1984.

Harris, Mark. *Henry Wiggen's Books*. New York: Bard, 1977.

Honig, Donald, and Larry Ritter. *The Glory of Their Times*. New York: Doubleday, 1981.

Jenkins, Dan. *Fairways and Greens*. New York: Main Street, 1995.

Rivers, Glenn and Bruce Brooks. *Those Who Love the Game—Glenn "Doc" Rivers on Life in the NBA and Elsewhere*. New York: Henry Holt, 1993.

Russell, Bill. *Second Wind: The Memoirs of an Opinionated Man*. New York: Ballantine, 1982.

Tunis, John R. *$port$*. New York: Dodd, Mead, 1928.

Great Strides
by Penny Colman

Colman, Penny. *Rosie the Riveter: Women Working on the Home Front in World War II*. New York: Crown, 1995.

Colman, Penny. *A Woman Unafraid: The Achievements of Frances Perkins*. New York: Atheneum, 1994.

Dubois, Ellen Carol, and Vicki Ruiz. *Unequal Sisters*. New York: Routledge, 1990.

Evans, Sara M. *Born for Liberty*. New York: Free Press, 1998.

Hines, Darlene Clark, and Kathleen Thompson. *A Shining Thread of Hope:*

A History of Black Women in America. New York: Broadway Books, 1998.

Moynihan, Ruth Barnes, Cynthia Russett, and Laurie Crumpacker. *Second to None: A Documentary History of American Women, Volume II.* Nebraska: University of Nebraska Press, 1993.

Weatherford, Doris. *Milestones: A Chronology of American Women's History.* New York: Facts on File, 1998.

The Changing Concept of Civil Rights in America
by Walter Dean Myers

Branch, Taylor. *Parting the Waters.* New York: Simon & Schuster/Touchstone, 1989.

Hughes, Langston, and Milton Meltzer. *A Pictorial History of African Americans.* New York: Crown, 1995.

Lewis, David Levering, ed. *W. E. B. Du Bois Reader.* New York: Henry Holt, 1995.

Williams, Juan. *Eyes on the Prize.* New York: Viking Press, 1987.

Fashioning Ourselves
by Lois Lowry

MacKrell, Alice. *An Illustrated History of Fashion.* New York: Drama Publishers, 1997.

Peacock, John. *Twentieth Century Fashion: The Complete Sourcebook.* New York: Thames & Hudson, 1993.

Politics—Not Just for Politicians
by Milton Meltzer

Brinkley, Alan. *Liberalism and Its Discontents.* Massachusetts: Harvard University Press, 1998.

Hobsbawn, Eric. *The Age of Extremes: A History of the World, 1914–1991.* New York: Vintage, 1994.

Meltzer, Milton. *American Politics: How It Really Works.* New York: Morrow, 1989.

Sullivan, Mark, and Dan Rather. *Our Times: America at the Birth of the Twentieth Century.* New York: Scribner, 1996.

Trust and Obey
by Katherine Paterson

Darwin, Charles. *The Descent of Man.* New York: Prometheus Books, 1997.

Darwin, Charles. *The Origin of the Species.* ed. Gillian Beer. New York: Oxford University Press, 1998.

Lawrence, Jerome, and Robert E. Lee. *Inherit the Wind.* New York: Bantam, 1982.

Paterson, John, and Katherine Paterson. illus. Anne Ophelia Dowden. *Consider the Lilies.* New York: Clarion, 1998.

Paterson, John, and Katherine Paterson. illus. Alexander Koshkin. *Images of Go.* New York: Clarion, 1998.

Heroes for the Whole Earth
by Laurence Pringle

Carson, Rachel. *Silent Spring* (25th anniversary edition). Boston: Houghton Mifflin, 1987.

Earthworks Group. *50 Simple Things You Can Do To Save the Earth.* California: Earthworks Press, 1990.

Leopold, Aldo. *A Sand County Almanac.* New York: Oxford University Press, 1964.

Pringle, Laurence. *Taking Care of the Earth: Kids in Action.* Pennsylvania: Boyds Mills Press, 1996.

Shabecoff, Philip. *A Fierce Green Fire: The American Environmental Movement.* New York: Hill & Wang, 1993.

INDEX